A ...

Tempting Fate

Kerrigan Byrne

Oliver Heber Books

PROLOGUE

Felicity Goode made certain she was alone in the hallway before she pressed her ear to the door.

It wasn't like her to eavesdrop.

But lately, she'd been doing all sorts of things out of the ordinary.

Today, her inquiry was one of a personal nature, and if she wasn't mistaken, she'd identified two masculine murmurs on the other side.

What she had to say needed no audience.

Before she could ascertain a single thing, the cool surface of the door fell away from her heated cheek.

It shouldn't have shocked her to find her brother-in-law Dr. Titus Conleith gripping the handle.

It was his office after all.

And yet, here she was, flustered to the point of speechlessness at the sight of his classically handsome features, arranged into a bemused expression.

"Felicity?" His brilliant whisky eyes flicked over her as if cataloguing a rudimentary clinical assessment. To her absolute discomfiture, the perplexed wrinkle beneath the chocolate forelock over his forehead deepened to a frown line. "Were you listening at the door?"

"I wasn't— that is— I'm not— you see, what transpired was—" A gather of guilt and nerves blocked her throat, forcing her to make an unladylike noise before she could speak in complete sentences. "I simply didn't want to disturb you if you were in a— private consultation." She peeked over his wide shoulder into his stately office.

He motioned inside as if gesturing to another. "Actually, I was consulting with—" Turning, he paused, scanning the length of his lair surreptitiously before his eyes narrowed. "With... myself, evidently."

"I see," Felicity nodded. Genius often coexisted with eccentricity, and Dr. Conleith was famously the most brilliant surgeon in the realm. No doubt he had to verbally manifest some of what resided in his brain into the world to organize it into coherence.

They stood in awkward silence, each obviously searching for the next thing to say.

As a little girl, Felicity had fancied herself in love with Titus Conleith.

He'd been a handsome, strapping stable boy at her father's estate, with a wide smile and wider shoulders. It wasn't only his gentle way with her painful shyness, or their shared love of esoteric and scientific literature that put her at ease.

It was that he never treated her like a moth in a family of butterflies.

Even though that was the reality of her life.

Her eldest sister, Honoria— whom they fondly called Nora— was the uncontested beauty of the Goode sisters. Then came Prudence, adventurous and lovely as she was lively, not to mention Felicity's own mischievous and magnificent twin Mercy, who was brilliant and bold and always wont to create loud— if entertaining— calamity.

More often than not, Felicity might as well be part of the furniture.

Titus had a knack for making people feel seen.

Alas, his heart had always belonged to Nora.

After consulting several romance novels on the subject of love and passion, Felicity came to the easy conclusion that her tender feelings for the man were more appreciative and filial than amorous.

Considering he was now her brother-in-law, it all worked out for the best. Still, though, she couldn't help but be tongue-tied in his presence.

Or anyone's presence, really.

Unlike the rest of the Goode girls, she was terrible at interaction.

"Was there something you needed?" Titus prompted gently, belying a curious tension whitening the hand holding the doorknob.

Taking in a deep breath, she nudged her spectacles up the bridge of her nose and smoothed at the waist of her pale blue bodice. "Might I… impose upon you for a moment?" She gestured expectantly at his office.

Fine lines branched from his eyes as he pasted on a smile too grand for the occasion. "No imposition at all. Do accompany me as I go to—"

"I'd rather speak in private," she said. "i-in your office, more specifically."

Why hadn't he invited her in? It wasn't at all like him not to be gracious to the point of indulgent.

He checked over his shoulder once more, as if hesitant, then slowly pulled the door wider, allowing her entry.

The undoubtedly masculine room might as well have been another world from the sterile atmosphere of the Alcott Surgical Specialty Hospital, over which he resided as chief of surgery. As fastidious as the man was with his medical implements, his paperwork was hopelessly disorganized. Strewn about in alarming disarray until one could only guess what his desk looked like.

The scent changed as she passed the threshold, no

longer sharp and sanitized, but soft and familiar. Comforting. Perhaps it was just the old books lining the many shelves, or the decorative and fragrant sachets of lavender she'd harvested herself from the glasshouse at Cresthaven Place. She'd had the idea to hang the sachets from the bronze velvet drapery cords.

This office was used to convey terrible diagnoses, the news of the death of a loved one, or possibly distressing information regarding procedures Titus was about to perform.

While volunteering at the hospital, Felicity had become convinced that the room should not only appear calming and friendly, but it should smell that way, as well.

Something else hung in the air today, though. Something sharper than the camphor-like scent of lavender. A watchful expectancy, perhaps. It seemed as if the motes of dust moved with more frenetic energy than the two of them warranted.

As if… the stillness contained some magnitude she identified but was unable to understand.

She felt suddenly exposed. Gooseflesh erupted everywhere, washing her spine in chills and tightening her nipples.

Glancing at Titus, she quickly ascertained the odd atmosphere wasn't at all emanating from him.

Then… what? The question certainly couldn't be *whom,* because they were alone.

So why did she feel the very devil's hot breath on her neck?

Rather than taking his post behind the desk, Titus leaned his hip against the edge as he gestured for her to sit in one of the comfortable velvet chairs facing him.

She declined with a tight shake of her head. "This shouldn't take long. I only have one question to ask of you."

Dark eyebrows drew down in an expression of concern. "Is this a question of a medical nature?"

"No—" She paused. "Well, yes, actually. Maybe... sort of?"

Once again, she was struck by how tense Titus seemed as his gaze skipped around the office rather than landing on her. "A sensitive medical nature?" he asked uneasily.

"Well, I came by to visit someone— a patient— but I'm unable to find him."

At that, Titus visibly relaxed. "To whom are you referring?"

Suddenly she felt rather itchy, and dug a finger into the tight coiffure beneath her hat to scratch at her scalp. "Um— please don't think me too inappropriate— but I thought to sit a while with..." The name was difficult to say. It wasn't the pronunciation she struggled with so much as the man who bore the name. He made her tongue feel heavy and unwieldy. "With Mr. Gabriel Sauvageau. I owe him my gratitude— or rather, I owe him my life. I understand he was injured during the violent chaos of the Midnight Masquerade at Killgore Keep whilst carrying me out of the fire. I was told he came here to seek treatment. I know it's been several days, and I should have come to call upon him earlier but..."

Felicity looked down at the carpet and did her best to rein in her galloping heartbeats. To control the breaths that threatened to become impossible as a vise tightened around her rib cage. She'd been concussed after a strike from a villain had felled her on the grand staircase, but the real reason she couldn't visit was because the world beyond her front doors had been too much to bear.

But she'd scraped her courage together today. And she'd been doing so well thus far. Could she not stave off the episode of terror just a while longer? Just until she discharged her duty and her conscience and thanked the man who saved her life.

A long, heavy sigh emptied Titus's lungs.

"Felicity." His eyes flicked down to the carpet, his expression troubled. "I'm sorry to tell you this but… Gabriel Sauvageau was shot by the villain Martin Trout. I… was unable to retrieve the bullet from his wound."

That bit of new information not only slowed her heart but stalled it completely. She'd met Mr. Sauvageau all but twice, and somehow felt as if the news of his demise was a violent blow to the chest.

"*What?*" she gasped. "That can't be. I was *there* when it happened! I— I distinctly remember watching Mr. Sauvageau walk away as if his injuries were not so serious… Did I not?"

Had she hallucinated?

After the murder of Mathilde Archambeau, a woman who'd come to her for help, Felicity had consented to join her sister Mercy at a Midnight Masquerade attended by London's elite. Not only were peers in attendance eager to debauch themselves, but so were the wealthy merchant class and the darlings of the *demimonde*. Actresses, authors, and academics mingled with marquesses, madams, and merry widows of the *haute ton*.

That night, among revelers had also been the royalty of the underworld.

The most notorious of whom were the Sauvageau brothers, Raphael and Gabriel, leaders of the smuggling gang who identified themselves as the Fauves.

Raphael was the suave and carnally handsome rake, and his elder brother, Gabriel, was a leviathan of a man who'd been so thoroughly disfigured he wore a mask in public.

When he went into public, which was almost never.

Apparently the Sauvageau brothers had been planning to leave behind their lives of crime, and because of it, their second in command, Marco Villanueve, had quite violently turned on them.

In the resulting fracas, Marco had mistaken Felicity for her twin and had taken her hostage to use her against Raphael, who'd fallen in love with Mercy.

"I… remember the gunshot," she breathed, walking through the terror of the moment in her mind. "Mr. Sauvageau did stumble and fall beneath the press of the panicking mob. But then he swept down the stairs and grappled with my captor, who sliced through his mask. I know I fainted after that… but there were moments of semiconsciousness where I remember being carried by Mr. Sauvageau through the burning building and out to the canal. I hear his voice in distant memory. I see his—his face." She broke off, struggling over a difficult swallow.

"Surely he could not have carried me so far if he'd been fatally wounded."

His face. His face had been the most terrible memory of all.

The poor man had no nose, no hair, an eye socket so damaged it barely deserved the term, and so many slices and scars on his face, it made speaking visibly difficult.

The sight had been horrific.

Heart-wrenching.

And cumulated with all of the horrors of the night, it'd been what brought on the infernal episode that'd overtaken her, and pulled her back beneath consciousness.

God, she was so ashamed of herself.

"Have I gone mad?" she whispered, pressing a hand to her forehead. "Did I imagine things?"

"You remember correctly," Titus said gently. "Mr. Sauvageau did indeed conduct you to safety. But people are capable of doing remarkable things in remarkable situations. Things that even seem inhuman or extraordinary. More often than not, pushing oneself like that when injured… it takes its toll."

Felicity covered her mouth. "Titus. Do you… do you

think he might have survived if he hadn't expended the effort to save me?"

Titus bucked his hip away from the desk and settled two careful hands on her shoulders. "Dear Felicity..." He seemed to choose his words carefully. "Things would not have ended any differently for Gabriel Sauvageau regardless of the circumstances. It's commendable what he did for you. I— I know he doesn't— he *wouldn't*— regret it."

Troubled, Felicity bit her cuticle. "Do you know where he's buried? At the very least I could pay my respects. Or make certain his headstone is properly done. Or perhaps plant something there in his memory."

"I don't. I could make inquiries."

"I'd appreciate that very much," she said woodenly. "I'll let you return to your business."

"Nora will come around for tea any moment, if you'd like to stay. She'd love to visit with you." Titus gathered up his white coat and punched his arms into the sleeves, indicating that he was going to the surgical theater.

"Yes, I'll— I'll go upstairs and wait, with your permission."

Titus and Nora Conleith resided in a lush penthouse above the hospital. Their home was one of Felicity's favorite places in all the world.

"You know our home is always open to you." Titus's face softened as he gave her shoulders a fond squeeze before releasing them. "It can't be easy, what with Mercy absconding with Raphael to the devil knows where, and your parents indefinitely retreating to the Riviera."

At this, Felicity gasped. "*Oh Lord.* Does Raphael know about his brother?"

Titus's lips tightened. "He and Mercy do know what became of him, yes."

"Poor man must be heartbroken. I understand they were close."

"Indeed."

"I'll write him my condolences when Mercy sends me a postcard from whatever port they next find themselves."

"That would be kind of you."

"Well..." Felicity's restless hands adjusted her spectacles, plucked at her collar, at the cuffs of her sleeves, at the watch dangling from a broach over her breast. "Good afternoon, Titus."

"Always a pleasure." He lifted her hand to kiss it.

The news of Gabriel Sauvageau's demise felt like a tragic end to an even more unfortunate life. He'd been so strong, so utterly large and impenetrable that it was almost impossible to imagine something so small as a bullet taking him down.

Though he'd been a smuggler and a criminal, even a man she'd once seen as a threat, he'd ultimately been her savior. After her assault, he'd held her like a child might cradle a porcelain doll.

One they were afraid of breaking.

He'd crooned gentle things into her ear in his native French, soothing her. He'd been frightening. He'd been criminal.

But... Someone had hurt him so abominably.

Someone had done all that terrifying damage to his face.

Felicity didn't allow her tear to fall until she'd turned away. Dashing it from her eye with her gloved hand, she fumbled with the door latch and slid back into the hospital's hallway.

Gabriel Sauvageau may have looked like a monster, but he'd always be a hero to her.

TITUS'S REVERENT WORDS FOUND GABRIEL WHERE HE'D ensconced himself behind the gently scented drapes. "I'm not a religious man… However, I can't help but believe you were meant to hear that."

Pushing the heavy velvet aside, Gabriel ventured back into the office, pathetically aware that he displaced the air Felicity Goode had only just occupied.

He took in lungsful of it, hoping to lock it away. Imagining that somehow, she'd become a part of him.

His heart felt two sizes too big for his chest, and it hurled itself against his rib cage as if seeking to escape and go after her.

All because he'd chanced a bold peek at her as she'd turned to leave.

And he'd watched a tear form like a gem on her fair lashes and slide down the perfection of her cheekbone.

For him.

Her grief, however slight, was both a waste and a miracle. It humbled and distressed him. And for her own sake, he could do nothing to assuage it.

He must stay dead to her, or all his plans would be for naught.

No one knew that everything he'd done since they'd met was for *her*…

Gabriel Sauvageau had been born to a ruthless, evil gangster. As much as he'd hated his father, known as *the Executioner,* he'd been in danger of becoming him.

He was the heir to the Fauve dynasty. Fauves meaning "wild beasts" in the language of his homeland of Monaco. His father, however, had been an exile from England.

Gabriel had been content to watch the empire that'd spawned his father burn to the ground with his help. He'd wanted to disassemble the city brick by brick, then light the spark that immolated everything.

Including the Fauves.

He'd been close to achieving his goal, too, until several months ago when the Goode sisters had found a cache of gold that'd been stolen from him.

He and Raphael had meant to take the gold back, but Mercy and Felicity Goode had proven themselves the better thieves.

Because they'd stolen the Sauvageau brothers' beating black hearts right out of their chests.

That night, Honoria Goode, Dr. Conlieth's bride, had been intent upon redemption.

Mercy Goode, the woman Raphael had recently eloped with, had been intent upon justice.

But Felicity, she'd only cared about those she loved.

She'd been shy, panicked, and yet she'd fought the most valiantly for a happy ending. Not only for Nora and Titus, but for everyone who'd been a part of that tense standoff between the Fauves and the law.

It was her impassioned plea for benevolence that'd melted some of the fortress of ice around Gabriel's heart. He'd made the decision then and there to give the gold to Titus and Nora in exchange for a favor.

A favor he currently collected upon.

Although most men joined a gang such as the Fauves for their own selfish or desperate reasons, Gabriel and Raphael Sauvageau never had that luxury. They'd been born to inherit their father's power, his fortune, and his enemies. What they hadn't realized until after their father had died, was the biggest threat to them was posed by their own men.

Beasts only followed whom they deemed worthy to lead.

A leader, once overthrown, was almost always devoured by the pack. Ripped apart by teeth and claw, or blade and bullets.

The Fauves were no different.

And so, Gabriel and his brother hatched a plan to fake their own deaths and abscond to distant shores with new identities, to enjoy the fortunes they'd amassed from profiteering off of the evil and the elite.

Who were, more often than not, one and the same.

Because Raphael had one of the most recognizably handsome faces in London, and Gabriel was possessed of equally identifiable but lamentably hideous features, staying in England was deemed too dangerous.

Establishing new identities and an escape plan had been effortless.

However— in the meantime— leaving Mercy and Felicity Goode had become an impossible task.

Raphael— now living as Remy Severand— was dashing and deviant enough to be able to sweep the adventurous Mercy onto a sapphic duchess's yacht to travel the world in luxury.

Whilst Gabriel stayed behind, lurking in the hospital as the genius surgeon crafted him an entirely new face during several complicated— and often experimental— procedures.

The plan was to meet his brother and sister-in-law in the West Indies, bringing the rest of their hidden fortune along with him by way of America.

But first... Gabriel had some unfinished business to take care of.

Finding the villain Marco Villanueve was paramount, as the man was the only one capable of keeping the Fauves at all organized in a way that might threaten the Goodes and their futures.

Eventually, Mercy and his brother might return to England, revealing the secret identities to Felicity.

He'd be long gone by then, having discharged his duty.

Gabriel caught a glimpse of his head in a decorative mirror on the office wall and winced. His healing flesh punished him with stabs and throbs of electric pain at the slightest motion.

After his third surgery, the bandages surrounding most of his head made him appear like a mummy... one who leaked blood and fluids from beneath his wrappings.

A secret fear spiked deep within his chest.

What if he was never anything but a horror to behold?

Dr. Conleith's voice broke through his bout of uncharacteristic anxiety.

"Like I was saying before, once the grafts above your brow and along your cheek are healed, speaking should be a great deal easier and exponentially less painful. Then I believe we'll finally be able to move on to crafting you a new nose."

He approached Gabriel cautiously, his brow furrowed. "It'll be the most painful procedure yet. I'll mold the skin from beneath your arm where, blessedly, you haven't any tattoos. But the skin will have to remain attached to your arm for blood flow. This means you'll spend weeks in bed with your head trapped to the side and your elbow lodged behind your head. I won't lie to you. The process will be— well— nothing less than excruciating."

Gabriel stared at the door through which Felicity had departed. If he'd been a kettle this morning, boiling with the pressure of boredom and unrelenting, agonizing pain, stress over the lack of news from his brother, and rage at Marco's betrayal...

He found himself quite distorted by her unconscious expression of gratitude. Instead of boiling over, he'd felt infused by fragrant tea leaves and rich cream to become something else entirely.

Her voice made him forget his throbbing head and itching flesh as it knitted together. The sight of her cooled his rage.

Her mere presence... soothed him.

What sort of woman could wield such magic?

"Mr. Sauvageau—" Conleith's patient prodding broke the spell, bringing him firmly back to the moment.

He'd murdered men for less.

Good thing he liked the doctor.

"I suppose I should start addressing you by your new identity, Mr. Gareth Severand."

He nodded his assent, as it would be good to practice being an entirely new person before he had to trot the man he'd become out in the world.

"I want you to listen," the doctor said with indisputable gravitas. "I do my utmost to save every life that comes through that door, though I'm patently aware that not every life is worth the effort. I am sworn to not consider myself the judge of that. However, I'm convinced that no matter what your sins are, your life is easily one of the most important that I've spared..."

When Titus Conleith's composure slipped, and he swallowed twice, Gabriel shook his head, intending to vehemently disagree.

"You can't convince me otherwise," Titus insisted, his voice a bit huskier with unabashed emotion. "If only for what you did for that girl." He nudged his chin toward the door. "Where my wife has often been considered the crown jewel of the Goode family, Felicity is like... a treasured rosebud. She's fragile and easily crushed. There are not many hearts in this world as pure and true as hers. I shouldn't like to think how broken— how indelibly shattered— everyone in this family would be if we lost her. We have you to thank for that."

Gabriel told himself he found it impossible to speak due to his healing wounds and not the tightness in his own throat.

For every moment he spent burning in hell, he'd have this to hold onto.

He'd saved Felicity Goode, because even heaven didn't deserve her.

CHAPTER 1

A YEAR LATER

There was simply nothing so dreadful as a day like today.

Felicity's empty stomach rolled and pitched as she used the back of her soiled glove to wipe a bit of perspiration from her brow, then below her eyes, and above her upper lip.

Sitting back on her heels, she surveyed the damage whilst doing her utmost to take in a deep breath. To keep her heartbeat from galloping away, crashing into her ribs with enough force to break them.

To swallow around the lump of absolute trepidation in her throat.

Puffing out a shallow breath, she ripped her gloves off and tossed them in the dirt, fighting the tears filling her sinuses and burning the corners of her eyes.

Usually, tending her garden was rather cathartic, but not this morning. It would be a miracle if her winter jasmine survived the month of May.

It would be an absolute marvel if *she* survived the afternoon.

With all she had to worry about, all she had to fear, Felicity was unable to fathom why the ruination of her memorial garden was the thing that threatened her composure.

Indeed, her tenuous grip on her sanity.

She'd been digging in the dirt since four o'clock that morning, only stopping when the dizziness compromised her balance. Or, when her racing heart threatened to explode through her chest, forcing her to sit on the ground and wait for the spell to pass or for death to take her.

It never did.

So, she'd have to face what the day brought.

Or, rather, *whom.*

So many people. Not people... *men.* She'd have to meet them all. Smile at them, be kind to them...

And then choose one. Which meant rejecting others.

What a nightmare.

Glancing around her iron and double-paned glasshouse at the array of blurred and vibrant color, she noted the sun had climbed higher than she'd realized.

Oh, that she could stay here amongst the dahlias and crocuses, the hyacinths and begonias. She much preferred their company to that of most people.

Pushing herself to her feet, Felicity stretched the stiff muscles of her back and reached for the pot of aloe vera. It'd been something of an experiment, as such things didn't tend to thrive in English soil, but she was determined to give it one more try in the house where the atmosphere was a little drier. Hopefully, she had time to get it inside for a triage, and return to tidy up the greenhouse and ready herself to face the day.

Carrying it gingerly with both hands, Felicity rushed from the hothouse into the courtyard of Cresthaven Place, her family's stately whinstone home in Mayfair. She found the courtyard entrance to the rear foyer locked.

After recent events, she'd instructed her staff to keep

all doors secured, and they must not have noticed she'd been outside.

It pleased her, though, that someone remained vigilant.

After knocking for several moments to no avail, she realized that the staff must be below stairs attending their own breakfast.

Which meant she'd need to go to the front entrance and ring the bell to summon her butler, Mr. Bartholomew.

Lifting her skirts, she scurried toward the deep courtyard arch— almost a tunnel— beneath which carriages passed through to unload their passengers away from the busy London streets.

The iron gate stood open in anticipation of the day's bevy of alarming traffic.

A familiar sensation poured over her, one that had plagued her for several months now. It was different than her general sense of anxiety and unease. Indeed, her flesh warmed and the fine hairs on her body would lift to attention. Immediately an alarm trilled up her spine as if her back had been licked by a demon.

She felt this sense most often at night, when she was alone. She'd go to her window and look out into the dark.

And was haunted by the sense that the darkness stared back at her.

Doing her best to ignore her trepidation, Felicity noted that one of the aloe leaves was broken, weeping its syrup-like substance. She balanced the pot in one hand and did her best to coax the bend of the branch back in without it snapping.

It might have worked, had she not crashed headlong into the wall.

The clay pot shattered upon the cobbles of her drive, leaving a strange little oblong mound of dirt upon which was strewn the single plant.

It absurdly reminded Felicity of a tiny grave. She made a silly sound of amusement as she blinked down at it with something almost like relief.

Well, there was no saving it now, and she was almost glad she didn't have to expend the energy.

She barely had any left.

Just as she reached down to tidy the pottery shards, the wall *moved*.

Felicity jumped back several paces, smothering a cry with her fingers as her brain slowly processed some facts she'd previously missed.

Walls were not broad and warm and covered in wool. They didn't smell of cedar chips and expensive tobacco.

And they certainly didn't have thick hair that gleamed like onyx glass.

With a horrified squeak, Felicity retreated several more paces as the impossibly wide man turned to face her.

He moved deliberately, she noticed, like a mountain or an ancient oak, as if taking care where he arranged his uncommon bulk in a world full of small and fragile things.

Normally, Felicity would be frozen on the spot, her mouth open like a demented fish as she searched her blank thoughts for something, *anything* to say to a stranger in these awkward and embarrassing circumstances. She'd be wishing the tiny grave between them was big enough for her to disappear into.

Perhaps forever.

She'd berate herself for her blindness, her clumsiness, and her inarticulate nature.

But something about the way the man stood in front of her, mute and quite unnaturally still, gave her the time to cobble a sentence together.

It seemed he, too, was frozen in place, stymied into silence by her inelegance.

"Oh, *do* forgive me for startling you, sir!" Though she'd put distance between them, she reached her hand toward him in a timeless gesture of *mea culpa*. "I wasn't minding my step. Did I soil your coat? Did I cause you any harm?"

She squinted over at him— or, rather, *up* at him— and yearned for her spectacles.

Because of the extremity of her nearsightedness, she had to stand indecently close to people to make out their features without optical assistance.

She'd have given anything for them now.

As it was, she could make out no more than an impression of the man rather than an exact vision of him. He was all darkness and brawn, like a storm cloud of strength even in the rare brilliance of this morning. She found it difficult to distinguish between the sharp black of his suit and coat and that of his hair, which meant he kept it longer than was fashionable.

His eyes were deep— too deep to ascertain color at this distance— his mouth charmingly crooked, his neck and jaw wide.

Felicity wanted to step closer, to truly take the measure of him. But to do so, of course, to a man to whom she'd not been introduced, would be the height of impropriety.

And people on this street watched her family for any misstep.

Especially since the myriad of scandals recently heaped upon their good name.

Upon the "Goode name," as it were.

"It is I who should beg your pardon." His reply rumbled in fathomless echoes over the stones with a depth she'd rarely before encountered. His accent was measured and cultured and only a little… off? Like he'd spent some time elsewhere besides London, and it'd imbued his speech with the barest exotic tinge she couldn't quite place. "I shouldn't have been lurking in your archway."

"Not at all," she rushed to soothe him. "*I* ran into *you*. I was trying to save my—" She gestured to the ruined aloe. "Well, it's not important. A lost cause, that. I'm spared aggravation and failure by this collision. I really should be thanking you."

He assessed her for a moment longer than was appropriate.

Felicity couldn't read thoughts from his blurred features, but an air of expectancy hovered in the silence. As if he waited for her to say something in particular.

She wished she knew what.

Then it struck her, and she put her hand to her forehead in self-reproach. Of course, he was the first of her plethora of meetings today.

"You're early, I think." She winced. "Or am I truly so late?" Her hand unconsciously reached for the timepiece on her bodice above her breast. Not finding it, she smoothed her palm down the line of her body. "My watch was somewhere— I *swear* I attached it to my apron when I— Oh drat! Have I lost it as well?"

He distracted her with a strangled sound, something between a cough and a groan. Instead of replying, he sank to his haunches and reached as if to gather up the shards of clay pottery at his feet. "I'll clear this and take my leave—"

"On no, please do not bother." She rushed forward and took his arm, tugging at it with both hands, gently urging him to stand.

It didn't escape her notice that she couldn't span the thickness of his arm with both hands. Nor that the muscles hardened to granite at her touch.

He didn't look up at her.

"This is easily swept into the bins," she encouraged further. "Follow me inside and let us talk in the parlor."

She sensed hesitation in him, and she released his arm, dismayed at her breach in conduct right out in the open.

Only when she gave him space did he stand, but he followed her as she led him to the front stoop.

"I'm not usually so prone to clumsiness," she lied, wondering at her innate need to explain her ineptitude to this stark and monumental stranger. "I've misplaced my spectacles somewhere in the glasshouse, you see, and I had an extra pair, but they were..." A wave of nerves gathered on the horizon, threatening to tumble over her, and she firmly forged on before it could wash her away. "Well, that story is rather why I'm in need of you."

"You need me to... help you find your spectacles?" He sounded genuinely baffled, and Felicity worried that he might be a little daft. His measured speech could connote a lack of cognition rather than an abundance of it.

"Tell me, are you here in answer to my advertisements in the paper, or did one of your colleagues I contacted refer you to me?"

"The paper..." His answer almost sounded like a question.

But at least he was literate.

Felicity climbed the eight steps to her grand door and pulled the bell that would summon her staff. "Did you bring references?" she queried, glancing back at him.

He lingered on the walk, one foot cautiously landing on the bottom stair. His hand gripped one of the points of the wrought iron gate, and she wondered if he could simply snap it in twain.

It was odd to have him looking up at her.

His hand went to his pocket. "I— do not have references on me."

Something in his voice tugged at her heart. Beneath his almost absurd profusion of brawn. Beneath the innate malice that seemed to roll from his shoulders in palpable waves. Even beneath the shards of gravel and glass in his sonorous voice.

Lingered a note she couldn't define.

It echoed from someplace so abysmal she might have imagined it. But to her, it felt like his every word— innocuous as they'd been— was laced with lament.

With fathomless desolation.

She had the strangest notion that this was quite possibly the loneliest creature she'd ever met.

Felicity had always been aware of what a ridiculous human she was. And yet, she stood in front of a dangerous man, awash with the same feeling she suffered when Balthazar, her ancient Labrador, silently begged for scraps of her supper.

"Do not let that distress you," she rushed to appease him. "I'm forever forgetting or misplacing things. We can still have our interview and you can give me your papers at a later time."

The door swung open and rather than her butler, it was young Billings, the coal boy, who blinked up at her. "What happened to you, miss? Are you all right?"

"Oh nothing, I've been in the garden and the rear entrance was locked." She swept inside and reached behind her to untie her apron and hand it to the lad. "Will you please summon Mrs. Winterton to chaperone my first interview of the day?"

"Mrs. Winterton inn't here, miss," the lad informed her. "She left a note saying she 'ad to take an early train north to see to her bruva… or was it her uncle?"

"Oh, dear. I hope it's not serious."

"Dunno, miss. Do you want me to summon Mrs. Pickering?"

Felicity looked over her shoulder to find the man had not followed her up the stairs. "Don't bother Mrs. Pickering from her breakfast, but when she's finished, she might join us in my personal parlor where I'll be making inquiries regarding qualifications for the position."

"Yes, miss." The boy scampered off, trailing the long ribbons of her apron in his wake.

She turned to the man who'd not moved from his spot. "If you might forgive the impropriety of the two of us spending a moment alone together, we could begin our conversation," she suggested. "My housekeeper will join us directly."

"Men like me have very little use for propriety."

The way he said that sent little shivers skittering along her skin. For some inexplicable reason, she hoped Mrs. Pickering didn't hurry her breakfast. Indeed, she found herself very much liking the idea of being alone with this man.

Which made absolutely no sense.

Felicity was possibly the most skittish woman of her acquaintance, especially in the company of men. And this one, this mountain of masculinity, was possibly the most imposing fellow she'd seen since... well, in at least a year.

She should be a catastrophe of disobedient nerves. But she wasn't.

At least, not more than usual.

If you would follow me, Mr...." As she swept over the marble floors toward her parlor, she realized she hadn't even asked his name.

"Severand. Gareth Severand." His answer came from closer than she'd expected.

My, but he moved swiftly and silently for a man of his size.

"I'm Miss Felicity Goode."

"I know who you are."

She let out a nervous chuckle. "Of course... of course you would know from whom you are soliciting a position-- how silly of me." She propped open the door to the parlor and gestured to a chair by the far window. "May I take your coat?"

"It's not necessary."

Felicity tucked into a chaise a very respectable distance apart from Mr. Severand, who folded himself into the wine-hued velvet chair with some caution, as if testing the structural dependability of the object before settling his entire bulk into it.

"Well," she began, abruptly losing what little confidence she possessed. "If I'm honest, I can't say I exactly know how to go about hiring personal protection."

At those words, he straightened, instantly more alert than before. "Let's start with why you need it."

"Right. Well… I erm…" She scratched at the hairline below her ear, smoothing at the tickle of hair as it stood on end.

She was alone with a dangerous creature, and her body knew it.

"As you may or may not be aware, my parents were the Baron and Baroness Cresthaven. They passed rather suddenly in a carriage incident on the Continent last year."

"I had heard. I'm sorry for your loss."

For a man who knew her not at all, he sounded remarkably genuine.

"Thank you. You are kind."

"I am not kind."

This was said so low, Felicity thought she might have misunderstood him. Or imagined he'd said it in the first place?

Deciding to let it lie, she continued. "Well, it turns out, before they left for the Riviera, my father amended his will. As he had no male heir, his title and the country seat of Cresthaven Abbey, of course, go to a distant cousin. But all my father's liquid capital, his shipping company, and various investments and holdings have been inexplicably bequeathed to me, of all people, with one very specific caveat."

"Which is?"

"Now that my year of mourning has passed, I must

marry into the aristocracy immediately. At the very least a viscount, or so the documents dictate."

She could feel, rather than see, his frown long before it was reflected in his voice. "Treacherous as the noble marriage market may be, I do not comprehend how I can assist you in that arena."

Felicity fiddled with the cuff on her sleeve, toying at the grey pearl buttons before pushing them through the little loops of midnight blue silk. "You are right. Of course you are. Finding a husband will be my lamentable responsibility, alone. But you see... the day before yesterday, I attended a lecture at Hornbrook Hall for the London Horticulture and Botany Society. The study was of night-blooming plants, so attendance was required late into the evening. The weather was pleasant when we adjourned, and I was overheated from the closeness of the room, so I decided to walk the handful of blocks here, rather than take a hackney." She swallowed over a lump in her throat and suppressed a tremor at the memory.

"Before I made it home, I was... accosted by a lone assailant." She pulled the cuff of one sleeve back to uncover the finger-sized bruises on her wrists.

Mr. Severand surged to his feet, knocking his chair backward.

"What the bloody hell was done to you?" The demand was not a roar like that of a lion, but more the low and lethal warning growl of a jaguar.

All the more penetrating for its resonance.

Astonished by his reaction, Felicity tucked her wrists into her body as if to protect them from his unanticipated rage. "Not very much, if I'm honest."

In the grand scheme of things, she'd been through worse.

"Tell me," he demanded.

"Well... he wrenched my arm and shoulder behind me and pulled at my— my hair." She smoothed at the back of her scalp where it still smarted. "He ripped my spectacles off and stepped on them."

With one hand, Mr. Severand jerked the chair upright, but he didn't claim it. Instead, he paced in front of the far window and stood like a sentinel against the sunlight. "What did he look like? Did he say anything? Where, *exactly,* in the city were you—?"

"Do sit down, Mr. Severand." She rushed to soothe him even as her own heartbeat accelerated. "It was not my intention to distress you."

His shoulders rose and fell with a tangibly difficult breath. And then he turned and reclaimed his seat as she bade him, though she didn't have to see the lines of his body to sense the palpable hostility emanating from him.

Perhaps answering his question would help.

"To be completely honest, I didn't get a good look at him. He told me that I did not deserve what I had. That he was going to take it from me. He sounded— a bit older. Not like an enfeebled elderly sort of fellow. But someone perhaps fifty or sixty. Mature and... and somewhat maniacal."

"Did he—" The sentence cut off as if his throat wouldn't allow him to say the words. "Did you suffer any other injuries?"

"No. Fortunately," she rushed on, compelled to appease him. "The brigand was frightened away by some rather drunken noble lads staggering from one sort of trouble to the next. He ran into an alley and disappeared."

When he said nothing, she continued. "I returned home that night, unbelievably agitated, only to find this." She extracted a scrap of paper from the pocket of her skirts, unfolded it, and set it on the table.

In that moment, the door clicked open, and a maid came in carrying tea and biscuits. She set it on the sideboard and curtsied. "Mrs. Pickering said she'd be up directly, miss."

"Thank you, Jane. Tell her there is no reason to rush. Mr. Severand and I are getting along quite well."

For some reason she did not dare identify, Felicity didn't want company other than his at present.

"Yes, miss." Jane glanced over at Mr. Severand and swallowed audibly. "I-If you are in need of assistance, ring the bell. Mr. Bartholomew is just outside the door."

This was obviously said for his benefit rather than hers.

"Thank you, Jane."

When Felicity turned back to Mr. Severand, she found he'd taken the paper and retreated to his seat to study it intently.

It was no epistle or manifesto, merely a sketching of Cresthaven Place engulfed in flames, with a chilling message printed hastily below.

I will claim what is mine.

"Do you have the envelope this arrived in?" he asked in a lethally subdued voice.

"That's just it," she explained. "It wasn't in the post. I found it on my personal correspondence secretary here in my parlor." She gestured to the desk in question, strewn with stationery and several of her favorite pens.

"Whoever left this was *in my house* and my staff witnessed *nothing*." She shivered as she did whenever the picture of the intruder invaded her mind's eye.

"This evidence suggests that my attack was not random violence, but something far more malevolent. Needless to say, I find personal protection necessary until I can secure a husband who's responsible for my safety. Since Parliament is in session, and my mourning for my parents is considered officially over, I'm expected to take a season. I-I need someone at my side so I can feel… so I *am* safe. At least until this enemy can be discovered and dealt with."

Felicity paused. Waiting for him to say something.

Wishing he were closer.

As a nervous sort of creature, she'd become a master at reading expressions, sussing out people's responses and emotions, if only to predict what their reactions might be at any given point so she could avoid conflict or worse.

Mr. Gareth Severand was not a man easily read, nor was he predictable. Even without her spectacles on, she was categorically certain of that.

"What about your family, Miss Goode?" he asked, still studying the paper in his hand. "Is not your brother-in-law a rather famous chief inspector at Scotland Yard? Has he seen this?"

Felicity glanced away, not for the first time wishing her family had not become so infamous through no fault of their own.

Well… almost.

"Chief Inspector Morley and my sister Prudence are abroad for a few weeks, settling my parents' final overseas interests. My eldest sister Honoria and her husband live above the Alcott Surgical Specialty Hospital. She's in her confinement with child, and is over thirty years. I'm told that makes pregnancy exponentially more difficult. I could never visit peril on their household or their patients. What if stress or danger caused Nora— that's what we call her— to lose the baby? I'd never forgive myself."

Felicity looked down at her lap, plucking a stray fiber off her dark frock. Tomorrow her new trousseau for the season would arrive, and she could put her mourning clothes away for a good long time.

"My sister Mercy…" Sadness drifted like a cloud over her heart, mingling with the love she felt for her twin. "She's on an extended honeymoon, and I can't say exactly where in the world she is at the moment. But I'm fairly certain she couldn't make it home in time to do any good, and I don't want to bother her…"

She glanced back in Mr. Severand's direction, noting that he'd folded the paper back up, but made no move to return it to her. "I-I did show that to a detective," she informed him. "He's the one who suggested I should engage personal security... so here you are."

"Here I am."

Was it her imagination, or did he sound none too happy about the prospect? Perhaps he didn't think he'd be a good fit for the job? Or maybe he could not be away from a family for so long?

"May I ask you a question, Miss Goode?" he queried, leaning forward in his chair.

"Certainly."

"Do you think your assailant meant to... to have his way with you?"

She swallowed and shuddered, but ultimately shook her head in the negative. "I can't speak to his ultimate designs, but there was nothing suggestive in his manner. Only violent. I know this sounds— well, I haven't much reference to pull from— but the attack felt personal. That man... he hated me. I didn't recognize him at all, but he *hated* me. He liked what he did to me. He enjoyed the fact that he could cause me pain and I was helpless against his strength."

"Doesn't seem possible," Severand murmured, turning his head away from her. "Someone hating you."

Something about the way he said that evoked a pleasant heat from beneath her collar to climb her neck and spread to her cheeks.

"Some people can hate you for just being born," she murmured, thinking of her father.

"That's true enough."

They shared a companionable silence. A discovery of a common pain, unspoken but already understood.

Felicity had known only a few men of close acquaintance. The first being her father, the Baron. A rotund bear of a man, his voice booming and his manners bombastic. He'd been overbearing, extremely religious, and unrelentingly critical. He'd had two loves in his life, money and power, and only paid his four daughters attention when he could use them to acquire more of one or the other.

To increasingly disastrous effect.

Even in death, the Baron controlled her future. Not with an iron fist, but an ironclad contract.

Her brothers-in-law were each of them good men in their own right. They had power or passion or both. They were protective rather than controlling, and adored her sisters with enviable devotion. Her family was so lively, and when they were together, the men and women spoke with equal fervor. There was laughter and debate, a multitude of opinions, and even more chaos.

Felicity loved it, and simultaneously felt lost in the maelstrom of it. Everyone spoke over each other, their wits firing like a volley of rifles, and their words often strewn about like projectiles.

She was often tempted to duck behind something to protect herself from them.

Though none of her loved ones aimed *at* her.

Not only because of her adversity to conflict, even harmless debate. But because she never said much in a crowd, preferring to watch the conversation rather than fight to be part of it. She was much more relaxed interacting as she did now, with one or two people, in a place that was comfortable and familiar.

All her own.

With someone who was capable of being silent long enough to let her gather thoughts often scrambled by nerves, like marbles spilled on a parquet floor. She'd spoken more to the man in front of her than to anyone else in a very long time.

And she found herself a little bit bold in his company,

which, considering his aura of general menace, was indeed a wonder.

"Mr. Severand," she inquired. "Would you consider yourself a violent man?"

He was quiet for a moment, shifting in his chair for the first time.

"Yes, Miss Goode. I am a violent man."

Felicity couldn't for the life of her understand why the way he said this caused little thrills of electricity to spark in her veins.

"Would—" She cleared something husky from her throat. "Would you go so far as to say that you... excel at violence?"

"I would go so far as to say it is the only thing I excel at."

"I see."

With that, she reached for the bell Jane had mentioned, and rang it.

Mr. Bartholomew appeared as if he'd been waiting on the other side of the door. "Do you need me to escort the — gentleman out, Miss Felicity?" He sniffed in the direction of her guest.

"No, Mr. Bartholomew, but, if you don't very much mind, I do need you to cancel my other appointments for today."

Small eyes beneath amusingly large eyebrows narrowed to a comical degree. "Are you quite certain, miss?"

"I am," she said, feeling more certain about this than she had about anything in a long time. "That is, if Mr. Severand accepts the job I am offering him."

CHAPTER 2

As Gabriel followed Felicity Goode through the grand manse he'd watched so often, he appreciated the enticing scent left in her wake. It was even better than he remembered, herbs and lilacs and honeysuckle reminiscent of the sun-drenched vines of his homeland in Monaco.

He could not believe she was close enough to touch. That he could simply reach out and…

No. He curled his hands at his sides.

He would never. Hands such as his would stain her.

His gaze touched her everywhere, though, cataloguing every delectable detail. The ridge of her corset beneath her fitted, solemn blouse. The arousing disarray of her hastily knotted hair. The careful set of her slim shoulders and the soft sway of her hips.

Blood no longer flowed through his veins, there was no room for it. He was a beast overwhelmed by so many opposing forces, he could barely contain himself.

A fury coursed through him so white and hot, it threatened to singe his flesh from the inside out. She'd bruises on her delicate wrists. A man had dared to grab her, imprison her. Frighten her.

A dead man, if he had anything to say about it.

Sheer befuddlement followed on the heels of said rage, as he tried to examine just how he'd found himself ambling after her on the lush, blue Egyptian carpets of Cresthaven Place, admiring her shape. He tried his utmost to pay attention to the tour, but he had a rudimentary familiarization with the layout. The rest was merely decoration where he was concerned.

When she was near, how could he admire anything else?

Christ, how was this happening?

Only moments ago, he'd been lurking in the archway that led from the street, hoping to catch a glimpse of her in the garden. Possibly his last before he left for the other side of the world.

The glimpse had been granted as she scurried from her glasshouse, that little pot cradled in her hands. He'd ducked into the shadows as she'd reached the courtyard door. Cautious of being sighted, he turned to go, grappling with a yawning sense of loss.

One moment he was cataloguing his final vision of her. The sheen of her hair, the heightened color of her full lower lip as it emerged from between her teeth. The elegant arch of her neck, at the base of which little fair wisps formed tight ringlets in the humidity of the hothouse.

And the next moment... she'd bounced off his back like an adorable beam of sunlight.

Gabriel had been speechless as he turned to see her gaping over at him. Even rumpled in a soiled apron and a streak of dirt dashed across one pale cheek, she was unutterably lovely.

Ethereal.

He'd been frozen with the fear that she'd recognize him. Even though he looked nothing like himself—nothing like the monster who'd terrified her a year prior. He'd spent the past several months perfecting an English accent. He'd allowed his hair to grow out for the first time in decades.

But he had other identifiable characteristics.

His height and breadth, for one. The depth of his voice. The color of his eyes. And a myriad of scars, albeit less severe ones, that still marred his features.

Felicity's eyes, blue as the Mediterranean, had glimmered with worry for him rather than approbation. She'd asked if she'd hurt him, and it was all he could do not to laugh.

Gabriel couldn't remember the last time he'd laughed.

It astonished him that she'd offered him the position while he bumbled around like a demented buffoon.

She couldn't possibly understand the effect she had on him. Didn't realize that her apology had been the first he'd received from someone not bleeding and/or about to die.

Nor that she was the first woman to ever reach for him of her own accord, let alone tug at his arm.

While he'd struggled to process that monumental occasion, she'd invited him into her parlor, and into her employ, before he'd quite understood what was going on.

He could choke on the bitter irony of the entire bloody situation.

After he and Raphael were reported to have died in a fire, Gabriel had lurked about Cresthaven Place for several months as he recovered from his multiple surgeries, telling himself he wasn't *watching* Felicity, but *guarding* her. He feared that Marco Villanueve, the man he had betrayed before he'd faked his death, would come to harm her, if only to get his revenge.

Gabriel had lied to himself for a while, convincing himself he was only looking after family. Raphael had married her twin, after all.

But he couldn't deny how hungry he was for a mere peek at her. For the barest glimpse of her golden hair as she swept from a carriage to her home. For the sound of her voice as she replied to a greeting from a neighbor.

As it happened, Marco Villanueve had disappeared from the face of the planet months ago. Everyone assumed him dead, run afoul of the underworld.

Cresthaven had been quiet and safe since her parents' deaths, as callers outside of the family were not allowed during mourning. Not to mention, Felicity had always been surrounded and protected by loved ones.

And so, after a long year, Gabriel could no longer put off fulfilling his promise to join his brother.

He'd lingered in the darkness too long, feeling a one-sided companionship when her lamp would go on at all hours. Knowing she couldn't sleep either, that dreams were not a safe place for her troubled mind. Wishing to hold and soothe her.

Wishing she would do the same.

On his favorite nights, she would pull the drapes aside and gaze out into the dark as if searching for something.

In his more pitiful moments, he'd fancy that something was him.

Just as Gabriel had promised to give up the deviant and obsessive proclivity of guarding her, of *watching* her...

She'd been attacked.

Whoever said irony was humorous could fuck right off.

Well, there was no chance he'd leave now, not until he made certain her world was safe once more.

Though, he'd help get her a husband over his own dead body.

Granted, to her he'd been dead nigh on a year now. And he had to remain that way, to keep her safe. Safe from his past. From his enemies. From his sins and his crimes and his consuming, nigh *demonic* need.

Her brother-in-law, Chief Inspector Carlton Morley,

had cautioned that if he caught Gabriel in London again, there would be no saving him from the noose.

Yes, he was bloody well aware he played a dangerous game venturing into her life.

Into her home.

This would be a treacherous lie.

Good thing he was used to danger. That he could think of no better death than one spent in service of her life.

But not before he lethally and efficiently dismantled anyone who threatened her.

Was he a violent man, she'd asked.

He was violence personified.

Which was why he could never be the man for her.

No, she'd marry a lord who could keep her cosseted in the society in which she'd been born. Who could offer her a name and a pedigree and all the gentility bred into the upper class.

Gentility he never even hoped to possess.

"You shouldn't have invited me in," he muttered as he followed her up the grand staircase. He would have protected her no matter whom she selected to employ. And as he watched her rear sway at eye level, he began to fear that spending any time in her company was a perilous mistake.

"Why do you say that?" she asked over her shoulder.

He cast about for an answer, not meaning to have spoken his thoughts aloud. "You haven't seen my references. Nor my skills. Your decision was hasty. I could be terrible at my job."

She snorted a little. "It's rather worse than that; I haven't even seen your face. But I believe you know what you're about, and that you are not the sort of man who would look for a position he could not fill. Besides, I imagine that your mere presence would prove a discouragement to trouble. Should anyone come at you, they'd break like waves on the rocks."

He grunted. That was true enough.

Wait... His brow furrowed. What did she mean she hadn't seen his face?

Out of habit, he brought his fingers up to check to see if the mask that had been a part of his life since the age of sixteen had somehow magically appeared affixed to his brow.

Though he'd been a year without it, he often still felt quite naked.

Exposed.

No. His features were bare, so why—?

Felicity's hip crashed into a delicately carved side table, sending an empty vase flying into the air.

Gabriel caught it and gingerly returned the delicate object to the table once she righted it again.

"Thank you." She huffed out an anxious giggle, turning away without looking at him, to press her hands against flaming red cheeks. "I really need to find my spectacles, or I'll be hopelessly blind for tomorrow night."

"What's tomorrow night?"

She heaved a soul-weary sigh. "Lady Brentwell is hosting a ball. It's my first foray back into society since my parents' deaths." She paused as if plucking a thought out of the sky. "I'm hoping you have formal wear, Mr. Severand. If not, Mr. Bartholomew is a more than adequate tailor in a pinch—"

"I'll send for some things," he clipped, liking the idea of the sour-faced Mr. Bartholomew attending him only slightly more than the ball he now dreaded with his entire being.

"At my expense, of course," she insisted.

Gabriel wanted to argue. He was without question the wealthier of the two of them, but could not say so if he intended to keep up this ruse. Instead, he examined their surroundings as they climbed to the third floor.

Cresthaven was a grand old place, the name as original as the dynasty that currently sat on the throne. It lacked some of the more modern amenities and popular Egyptian and East Asian influence in décor, hailing back to a more medieval aesthetic that evoked the gothic feel of Barcelona. Heavy tapestries did little to muffle the sounds of their footsteps on the marble floors, nor the creaks of the ancient grand staircase.

The opulence was undeniable, however, in the crystal tinkling beneath the gas lamps, and the expensive statuary lining the halls.

"These windows over the garden trellis should be locked, as the structure could be easily climbed," he noted aloud. He'd watched his brother do that very thing, and sneak into Mercy Goode's bedroom to have his way with her.

"The washroom skylights should be secured, as well." He pointed at the doors, doing his best not to think of any sort of sex happening in this house, lest his body stir.

Never. *Not. Ever.*

"How did you know those were the washrooms?" she queried, moving to secure the window latches.

Shit. He couldn't very well say that he noted the tenants of the house carried lamps in the night to visit this very spot, only to return to their rooms. "Erm, many of my employers have been in this borough; the layouts are often the same in these houses."

"Oh, of course, I never thought of that." She accepted his answer with blithe naiveté, and part of him hated that someday, learning the truth about him would teach her to be more cynical. To distrust and to suspect.

Innocence never lasted long in his world. He hated that it would dilute hers as well.

Her life, though, was a worthy trade.

"Here's your room." She opened a door and stepped aside, giving him a wide berth.

"My room?" He peered into what was, even to him, a palatial accommodation done in masculine shades of green and bronze. "Shouldn't I bed down in the servants' quarters?"

"The servants' quarters are all occupied, I'm afraid, and they're also very far away from my chamber, which is just there." She motioned to the next door over. "Seeing as how the interloper made it into the house, I… I'd rather you were close by."

Gabriel was not a man prone to panic, but it rose within him now. There would only be a wall between them.

This was a perilous fiction. He could— he should— confess everything right now.

I'm Gabriel Sauvageau living as Gareth Severand. You've seen my ruined face. You've been terrified of me before. Having me beneath your roof might prove more dangerous than if I left you alone.

Because I am a violent man, and other violent men want me to remain dead.

They'd try to tear you apart just to make me watch.

And then you'd meet the real me.

The one drenched in blood.

No, best he stayed a dead man. A distant memory. Someone she could say a polite fare-thee-well to when the time came. He could slip back into the lonely shadows, leaving her in the light where she belonged.

The fact that her family— that her own twin— hadn't confided the Severand names to her made it clear that they also wanted their sister protected from the truth. At least for now.

Christ, this was complicated.

Something she'd just said permeated the maelstrom of

his thoughts. "Wait... you have a full servants' quarters? A full staff, only for you?"

"Well..." Her lips twisted in adorable chagrin. "I couldn't let any of them go, could I? Not when I could afford to keep them. It's not their fault Cresthaven emptied out rather quickly. First Nora, then Pru, Mercy, and my parents... The staff rely on me for income. Should I put out the second cook who is raising her grandchildren? Or perhaps Heather, one of our upstairs maids, a widow who cares for her ailing father? Or Mrs. Winterton, who was once my governess, but is recently orphaned and destitute. Why, she pays for the schooling of her younger sister. I'd be a monster to let her go."

"But have they anything to do?" he queried.

"Certainly." Her eyes shifted as she searched her thoughts for an answer. "I mean... our silver has never gleamed so brightly, and I challenge you to find a speck of dust."

Lord, but she was kind.

Her exceedingly gentle heart was what had set her apart from her twin in the first place. Mercy Goode was like a storm, whirling about with a charming and brilliant chaos that endlessly entertained and enchanted his brother.

Gabriel liked the woman, there was certainly no reason not to, but he was *tired* of chaos. His life had been one hurricane after another. One long and endless battle surrounded by subordinates equally as dangerous and untrustworthy as enemies.

Felicity was a cool and quiet breeze in contrast to her sister's bluster. The gentle rustle of leaves, the swish of long grass, and the flap of a hummingbird's wings.

She was the music that one must be still and quiet to hear.

And he appreciated her all the more for it.

Her heart was as large as the black hole swirling in his

own chest, and he often wondered what it must be like to care so much. To feel so deeply. To love with such unabashed confidence.

Such trust and grace.

The self-conscious clearing of her throat made Gabriel painfully aware that he'd been contemplating her in silence for much too long.

"Well, here I shall leave you to be settled..." She tucked a stray tousled ringlet behind her ear.

"Miss Goode, I—"

"Would you join me for dinner at half eight? I would like to discuss the particulars of my— *our*— upcoming schedule for the season. I'm certain you'll find it exceedingly tedious, but—"

"Yes." He'd listen to the *Iliad* read in its original language if only to share a meal with her.

"Excellent. Good afternoon, Mr. Severand." She held out her hand, though her timid gaze didn't lift above his vest.

That was twice in one day she'd reached for him.

Holding his breath, he took her hand, afraid to put any pressure on the tiny bones of her elegant fingers. He shook thrice, forcing himself to let them go with an unstable exhale.

She directed a winsome smile at his cravat, and scurried away.

Gabriel shut the door and leaned against it, suddenly feeling as if he'd been released from some sort of velvet rope. A manacle chaining his body to hers. She could have walked him like a hound, and he'd happily submit to her leash.

She was going to destroy him. That's all there was to it.

God. Why hadn't he taken Raphael up on his advice to pay for a woman's touch so long ago?

Regardless of what his face used to look like, he could

have had a strumpet in the dark, he could have... done any sort of thing, really. And if he had, maybe the mere press of Felicity's hand wouldn't have him tied up in absolute knots.

He curled his fist around the ghost of her grip, savoring every whorl and ebb of gloveless fingertips.

"Cheever," the trill of her sweet voice rang from down the hall. "Could I trouble you to check in on Mr. Severand? He'll need to arrange for his things to be brought for an extended stay."

"Of course, Miss Felicity, and I'll set him a place in the servants' hall for supper."

"Actually, he'll be joining Mrs. Winterton and me for dinner; we'll have much to discuss."

"Very good, miss."

Could I trouble you... Who spoke to their servants in such a way?

Felicity Goode.

Looking around the guest room, he felt so strange... he was in her house. Inside the very place he'd watched for so long in the golden glow of the windows as he stood outside in the cold.

He'd have to remember not to get comfortable here. As soon as he put the severed pieces of the bastard who threatened her into the ground, he'd disappear.

All he had to do was keep himself from killing the lucky blighter she selected to marry.

CHAPTER 3

Many people had accused Felicity of burying her face in a book, but in this instance, it was true in the literal sense.

The search for her spectacles in the hothouse had been unsuccessful, and she hadn't wanted to bother anyone else by asking them to hunt for her. She'd simply have to go to the optician and purchase a couple of new pairs.

When a delivery cart arrived with a few sparse trunks for her intriguing new employee, she did what any self-respecting lady of the house might do…

She hid in her parlor to avoid having to meet anyone.

As pitiful as she was, she could only summon strength for so many strangers in a week's time, and Gareth Severand took up a lot of space. Not only in the physical sense, but also more indistinguishable ways. It was as though she could feel where he stood beneath her roof, like a shadow in the walls.

This awareness both enthralled and exhausted her, and she had to save herself for the torture that was tomorrow's impending ball.

When her parents were alive, she'd not been allowed

to read novels, so she and Mercy had sneaked them from libraries and friends' houses.

But now she could keep them in the open on her very own bookshelves, and escape into the world of Fabian and Maryanne as they explored their passions on the high seas.

She draped herself on the chaise by the fire, one foot propped on the seat and the other on the floor as she reclined on a tufted pillow.

Even if she had recovered her spectacles, Felicity suspected she'd have held the book just as close to her eyes so her mind could absorb the words in a whisper. Each paragraph was so mortifyingly, titillatingly scandalous, she often had to peek around to make certain no one knew the debauchery in which her thoughts were absorbed.

Fabian, a reprobate and a pirate, was stalking the prim and proper Maryanne. Not cornering her, per se, but wickedly seducing her.

Relentlessly enticing her.

And even though he'd stolen her from her betrothed, the handsome but villainous Duke of Rottersham, Maryanne had just succumbed to Fabian's ravishing kiss.

Felicity's own lips parted as the scene came to life in her mind. A windswept sea. A man-o'-war bearing down upon the woman who would make this villain her lover.

And a kiss that was both forbidden and unholy, sealing their fates and their hearts together.

Every time Felicity encountered such a scene, her ever-tense muscles seemed to both awaken and melt. Inside, her body became both liquid and sharp.

Several sensations twisted inside of her all at once.

When Fabian ran his fingers over Maryanne's lips, Felicity echoed the motion on her own mouth, tickling the edges of the sensitive nerves with her fingertip. Agitated, she drew her touch down her chin and the delicate skin of her throat, then fiddled with the braiding at her bodice, right above her tightened nipples.

Even her hair seemed to stand on end as she smoothed down the silk panels of her ribs, now lifting with the quickening pace of her lungs.

Her hand hesitated on her belly and her thighs clenched as she gorged on words both carnal and confounding.

Here the descriptions became flowery and opaque... the entire scene eventually fading behind a closed door.

The book mentioned that Fabian had used his hands and mouth to create inevitable spasms inside of Maryanne.

Inside? With his mouth?

Certainly, Felicity understood the allegorical depictions of carnality between men and women. The mechanics of it. She and Mercy had stolen numerous medical texts on anatomy from Titus, and then she'd done her level best to fill in the gaps with her own romantic literature.

But what did this mean? What could a man's mouth do to a woman's insides?

Perhaps she'd work up the bravery to ask Nora...

Except she didn't want to picture any sort of wickedness between Nora and Titus. The very thought made her clap her hands over her eyes and groan with unnecessary chagrin. If Mercy were here, *she'd* be bold enough to ask anyone.

Maybe she knew herself, now that she was married.

Maybe... if Felicity found a husband she liked, she could ask him to show her.

The idea made her entire belly flop over with a squeamish yet giddy anxiety. She draped the entire book over her face, inhaling the familiar fragrance of paper and ink dusted with age and perfumed with the pressed tea rose she used as a bookmark.

Oh, but she couldn't take it. It was too much. Too delicious. The very fibers of her muscles seemed to be alive. Awake and aware in a way they'd not been before today.

Perhaps because, in her mind's eye, Fabian had adopted a very real shape. The descriptions of his dangerous masculinity. Of his threatening posture and his graveled voice and wealth of long, dark hair... well, she couldn't help but superimpose Mr. Severand's general presence onto the man.

It wasn't like he would even know, she justified to herself.

And she'd not done it on purpose or anything, she'd just begun reading and— there he'd been, looming in her mind's eye.

Felicity felt flushed and feverish, and fought a familiar disquieted sensation. One she often felt on sleepless nights when she lurked at her window, looking out into the dark.

As if haunted by longing, plagued by a yearning that did not entirely belong to her.

Or maybe it did, what did she know?

Taking one last enormous breath fragranced by her book, she lifted it from her face and let out an embarrassing squeak as the enormous shadow in the doorway startled the tar out of her.

Limbs flailing, she managed to struggle into a proper sitting position, a bit flummoxed to be caught in such a strange and inappropriate posture. Reclined with one leg bent.

"Oh! Mr. Severand... hello." She smoothed at her hair, her dress, crossed her ankles and pressed her thighs together against *that* place, hoping to be able to ignore a strange pulse there whilst in his presence.

No such luck.

"Goodness, forgive me! I was... lost in a book and forgot that I'd left the door ajar."

"Lost?" he echoed in that dark, low timbre that did little to settle the tumult in her belly. Or lower. "It seemed to me you were actively trying to crawl inside it."

"How I wish I could," she chuffed breathlessly. "It's ever so interesting in there, and I have so many unanswered questions."

As he stood across the room in the doorway, she could more sense than see his discomfiture.

"Have you... changed your mind about supper?" he asked.

"What?"

Shifting, he drifted past the threshold only a few steps. "It's three quarters past eight, Miss Goode. I wondered if you'd rather reschedule—"

"Oh! Oh dear." She popped to her feet and spun this way and that, searching the table, the chair, and the carpets for her bookmark. "No, of course, we'll have dinner directly. You must be starving. I still haven't recovered my watch or my spectacles so I'm barely a functioning human being." She could have sworn she left the pressed flower on the arm of her chaise.

"Might I help you find something?" he offered.

"No, thank you." She peeked behind the settee, finding it frustratingly clean.

"Does your staff not alert you to the meal?"

"They must have forgotten..." She crouched to her knees, searching beneath the chaise, to no avail.

"Is that something your servants are allowed to do? Forget you?"

She stood, shaking out her skirts. *Oh, there it was!* Somehow, it'd been trapped in her petticoats. Good thing she'd thought to preserve the blossom in wax parchment or it would have disintegrated.

"I don't run a very tight ship, I'm afraid," she admitted with only a little chagrin as she reluctantly placed the bookmark against Fabian and Maryanne's amorous encounter. "The very idea of admonishing my staff causes me— well, I wouldn't even know how to do it, if I'm honest. Usually, Mrs. Winterton takes care of such things, but I don't know if she's returned from seeing to her family. As you can tell, the day quite got away from me."

He stared at her for a moment, and she read an alarming amount of disapproval in the lines of his posture. The man had dressed for dinner, she noted with approval, donning a white tie, gloves, and waistcoat beneath a jacket large enough to engulf two of her at least.

His tailor must charge extra for material.

"Your companion abandons her post on such a day, without a by-your-leave?"

Felicity puffed out her cheeks. It did sound rather amiss when he said it like that. "She knows I would grant her any leave, especially when a family member is involved."

Quick steps clacked down the hall as young Billings hauled coal to set by the fires for the night.

Mr. Severand turned and filled the doorway, effectively halting his progress. "Is your mistress's evening meal prepared?" His question was not a demand or a reproach, but when Gareth Severand spoke— even in such sonorous tones— the authority in his voice was unquestionable.

"It's um… I'll 'ave to check," Billing's voice squeaked from that place in between boyhood and youth.

"What industry are you and the rest of your staff in?" Severand asked mildly.

"Service, sir."

"And whom do you serve?"

"Miss Goode, of course. She's the lady of the 'ouse."

"Then are the staff, as people employed in service, fulfilling the obligation for which they are being recompensed?"

"N-not at present, no." As the boy still stood in the

hall, she couldn't see his face, but his voice wavered and cracked with shame. "I-I did bring her coal for the fire... that's my duty, sir, not the kitchens. I'd not see Miss Felicity go cold. Not me. Not *ever*."

"Indeed. At least you're a good lad." Mr. Severand stepped aside to make enough room for the boy, who tiptoed past the threshold to her parlor.

Scurrying to the fireplace, he abandoned the coal on the hearth and bowed to her.

Twice.

"Forgive the late hour, Miss Felicity. I am confident dinner is being prepared for you directly. But if not, I'll give 'em a right kick in the chops, see if I don't. You shouldn't go 'ungry."

"I very much doubt a kick will be necessary, Billings, but thank you for checking on their progress." She almost pitied the boy as he scooted out of the room, giving Severand a wide berth.

The man in question stood straight as a royal yeoman. "Forgive me if I was too bold, but it's important that you are fed. That you maintain your strength, especially considering the stress you've been subjected to."

She lifted a shoulder, oddly touched that her nourishment meant something to him. "You saved me from having to be bold. And, if I'm honest, I *am* rather hungry."

Finding his presence intense after she'd only just caught herself harboring inappropriate thoughts about him, Felicity turned to her bookshelf, sliding her novel in its place.

"May I ask what you were reading?" His question was cautious, almost shy, which stymied her.

This man had an air of someone who asked permission from no one. He was built roughly, with barbaric dimensions. He addressed her staff with unerring composure and confidence.

Even when he moved, it was with the motions of a

man who claimed the ground he stood upon and dared anyone to challenge that claim. Who owned and carefully chose his actions to flawless effect.

Addressing her, however, seemed to cause him a bit of bother.

"I'm reading *The Gilded Sea* by Daphne Crane."

"I've not heard of that one," he admitted, again sounding oddly sheepish.

Damned if it didn't charm her.

"It's a romantic adventure," she pressed on. "I'm positively absorbed."

"That was evident."

How long had he watched her? Felicity's mouth dried at the thought. Could a man as observant as he have noticed the wicked effects her novel wrought upon her?

"A-are you much of a reader, Mr. Severand?"

"I'm voracious."

That word. In that voice. *Dear Lord.* She sank back to the chaise, pressing her thighs back together and folding her hands over her lap to keep from squirming.

What was *wrong* with her?

"What-what is it you read?" she queried, hoping he'd take the conversation so she could recover some of her wits.

"I like a bit of adventure, myself. And comedy. Satire. Notably, Hugo and Verne. Most recently, Wilde."

"Oscar Wilde?" she exclaimed. "I have heard he's working on a new play. Do you have plans to see it?"

"I've… never been to the theater."

"Oh." She didn't know what to say to that. Though he seemed dressed rather well, it was altogether likely that the theater was a luxury he might not afford.

He said nothing. And she cast about to fill the silence.

"Might I offer you an aperitif, Mr. Severand? Brandy, perhaps?" She stood, happy to busy herself at the sideboard.

"Do you have cognac?"

My, he said that word with such a flare. She wondered if he knew French.

What an enigma this man was.

"Indeed." She took the decanter and uncorked it, trying not to seem too curious.

Too eager.

Because she was.

"Tell me a little about yourself, Mr. Severand. This job isn't taking you away from a family, I hope. A wife? Children?" She poured him a generous drink and splashed some into a glass for herself.

She'd never tried cognac before. It wasn't done for females to partake in polite society. But something told her Mr. Severand wouldn't like to drink alone.

And wouldn't judge her if her choice in libation matched his own.

"No family." The tone of his answer could have dried up the Nile.

Beneath a pang of sadness for him, was a distressing little spurt of relief. She'd not like the idea of taking a husband away from his spouse and children to spend his days— his nights— with her.

Yes, better that he *not* have a wife.

She much preferred that.

Felicity set his drink on the table, strategically knowing that he'd have to peel his back from the wall and sit across from her in order to drink it.

"Please." She motioned to the chair he'd occupied earlier, before settling herself in her chaise across from him.

He took his seat just as carefully as before, leaning forward to claim the drink and tossing it back in one mighty swallow.

Felicity sipped at hers, blanching a bit at the startling burn. It wasn't at all unpleasant though, as the heat spread across her tongue and down her throat, lingering for several moments.

The aftertaste reminded her of baked apples.

"Miss Goode," he hesitated. "I can't help but wonder why you engaged my services without speaking to the other applicants for comparison. The choice seems..."

She mentally catalogued all the words he didn't say. Idiotic. Ridiculous. Impetuous. Foolish.

Sighing, Felicity abandoned her drink for a moment, needing to recover from her initial sip. "I suppose I should warn you of this before you learn it on your own. I am... an infuriatingly absurd woman. I often find myself irrationally fearful in the presence of strangers. In fact, I've dreaded this day since I posted the advertisement, because I'd have to meet with so many new men— er— people. The very thought exhausted me. I didn't sleep one wink last night."

"That doesn't make you absurd, especially considering your recent ordeal—"

"That's just it." She changed her mind and retrieved her glass again, taking a bolder sip than before. "My attack has little to do with it. I've always been this way."

His grip tightened on his glass, and he leaned forward a little, clarifying the impression of dark, deep-set eyes and a serious mouth. "What are you afraid of, Miss Goode?"

She released a wry sound from the back of her throat. "I fear nothing of consequence and everything beneath the sun. Saying the wrong words, for example. I dread the trivial and the inevitable, such as appearing silly and weak in the presence of gruff and capable men." She motioned in his direction with a wry smile.

She ticked her fears off on her finger. "I fear the improbable, such as the sky falling or the streets flooding, or being hit by lightning in a storm. I fear losing those I love the most, even though that's unavoidable. I fear dying. I fear living. Most recently, I fear that someone might burn my house down with me still inside it." She paused, clearing a gather of emotion from her throat so she could bring the moment a bit of levity. "Yesterday I most feared that the sheer breadth of my ridiculousness would be revealed to my future personal guard, and here I am exposing it to you voluntarily."

"You're saying… hiring the first man who appeared on your doorstep saved you from that torment." He didn't state this as a question, but she heard one beneath the words.

Felicity plucked at a seam in her skirts, carefully considering her answer. "I hope you'll forgive my forwardness, but that isn't at all what I was getting at. I hired you because… because even though you startled me when we met, you didn't frighten me."

"I… don't follow."

She wasn't certain she did either, but here they were. She was about to make herself vulnerable to his ridicule and somehow, she didn't care.

She wasn't afraid. For once.

"There is something about your presence, Mr. Severand, that I find comforting. And with a nervous disposition like mine, a reassuring presence is like a rare treasure, indeed. *That* is why I engaged you on the spot. I… felt immediately safe with you."

He didn't answer for a beat longer than she expected. "But… I told you I am a dangerous and violent man."

"And, as it happens, I am in need of a dangerous and violent man."

He sat stock-still but for his shoulders lifting and lowering with what seemed like labored breath. He said nothing. Just remained immobile for an increasingly unsettling length of time.

"Does that… Did what I revealed bother you?" she worried.

He set his glass down and stood abruptly, retreating toward the window, beyond which a misting rain dimmed the light of the streetlamps. He stared out into the darkness for a moment, and Felicity absurdly wondered if he yearned to be out where he belonged.

Because he was part of that darkness.

He marched toward the door, and just as she feared he was about to leave, he shut them in and strode back to the adjacent window. "Before we go any further, Miss Goode, I need you to look at me."

Stymied, Felicity stood, as well. Was he going mad? "I *am* looking at you."

"Can you see my face?"

Oh. That. "Not… in exacting detail."

"You should, before you invite me to attend you in public." His voice never lifted in volume or octave, but it was threaded with increasing tension. "I do not fit comfortably into a ballroom or a lady's solarium. You might regret asking me to. I will stand here, and you can approach at your discretion."

"I don't see why that's necessary—"

"Just… come closer." His tone took on an edge, but was also weathered by something she might have identified as dread mixed with a resigned exhaustion.

"Please," he amended more gently.

"Very well. If you insist." Felicity was equal parts curious and cautious. She thought Daniel might have experienced something like she did as he braved the lion's den.

Unafraid, but very aware what sort of beast she approached.

He could devour her whole, but she knew he wouldn't. At least, she was *fairly* certain.

She didn't stop until she stood before him, her head tilted back as his bent down to grant her unrestricted access to examine him.

He stood like a statue, like an effigy of some ancient

Roman general beneath her gaze, and Felicity was certain he didn't even breathe.

It became instantly apparent what he'd meant for her to see.

What he feared she would revile.

His face was a monument to violence. Indeed, a map of it. His nose crooked and dented, as if it'd been broken too many times and then cobbled back together. A slash interrupted his bottom lip. Another, his brow. A few more disappeared into his hairline, which was so black it gleamed blue in the candlelight. His left eyelid closed slightly more than his right, granting him an eternally malevolent glare. Some of the skin on his left cheek appeared glossy and tinged just a little pinker than the rest of his weathered, craggy features. Deep grooves bracketed a hard mouth, which was pressed into a hyphen and whitened at the corners.

He was too brutal to be handsome. His jaw square and wide, his chin strong and sharp. The hollows of his cheeks were deep as canyons and the skin beneath his eyes bruised from sleepless nights, creating a starkness about him that threatened to break her heart.

But it was his eyes she couldn't look away from.

They weren't dark as she'd first thought, merely set deep into a heavy brow and rife with shadows.

The gaze he affixed onto her was a mercurial silver/grey. The striations within the irises might have held some green and gold if he stood in the sun. Transfixed by their beauty, Felicity found it impossible to identify what she read in those eyes. No word existed in her vocabulary to do so, but it tugged at her with an aching intensity.

His expression could have been cast from marble, and yet it was wary and prepared, as if he expected her to strike him. Or spit upon him.

Or scream and flee.

Perhaps some people had done.

Unexpectedly, her fingers itched to explore his compelling face. To smooth over his brow and draw a thumb over the pinkened skin of the long scar.

What unimaginable pain he had endured.

A strange, dark part of her hoped he'd answered in kind.

That out there, someone else was just as broken.

Dismayed by her uncharacteristic ferocity, Felicity became suddenly aware of how warm his breath felt on her skin, feathering over her cheeks in apple-scented puffs. Indeed, warmth emanated from every part of him, and the recognition struck her with bewildering force that beneath his elegant clothing and inelegant features, Gareth Severand was a *man*.

An incomparably large man with expanses of flesh and muscle so diametrically opposed to her own, she couldn't fathom what they must look like. What it must *be* like to move through the world as he did. A tower of strength and skill and scars.

She almost envied him.

As someone so consistently aware of her own vulnerability, she was struck with awe by his apparent invincibility.

This man fascinated her.

"Look your fill before you make up your mind." His voice was strung as tight as a bowstring, and his eyes focused on something behind her, as if he could no longer stand to meet her gaze.

"Dear Mr. Severand." She put a hand on his arm, hoping to convey a modicum of comfort. "Be at ease. My mind was quite made up this afternoon. Your features have nothing to do with it. If anything, I should think you appear as though you wouldn't hesitate to do your job. I'm more convinced of that than ever."

He stared at where her hand rested just above his

elbow as he quietly said, "There isn't a force in this city that could go through me to get to you."

He was being hyperbolic, of course, but for some reason she believed him.

Releasing his arm, she touched her own cheek, both glad and guilty to find nothing there but smooth, unbroken skin.

"Did this all happen whilst you protected someone else?"

"Yes." His gazed followed her hand with the intensity of a hound begging to be fed.

One of them should have pulled back. There was no reason for him to be standing over her like this. Or for her to tilt her head up a little higher. To step one inch closer. But some spell held her in a strange thrall, blocking out all visceral details that didn't have to do with him.

If he should press his lip to hers, would she feel the deep groove of the scar there? Did his mouth taste like hers did? Like apples and heat?

The door burst open to admit the efficient whirlwind that was Mrs. Emmaline Winterton, her red hair disheveled, the feather in her smart peach cap drooping, and copper ringlets heavy with rain.

"Please pardon my tardy return, Felicity," she demanded. "I was detained on the bridge as a cart full of bees— of all the ridiculous creatures— had quite tipped over and bogged everything up! Blighty little beasts went everywhere, and we ran for our lives through rivers of honey. Just look at my hem." She lifted a hem that did, indeed, appear sticky, baring a lovely ankle boot and a good part of her stockinged calf in the process.

Having hopped away from her scandalous proximity to Mr. Severand, Felicity looked up to ascertain if he'd noted— or appreciated— her companion's stockings.

Astonishingly enough, his eyes hadn't left hers yet,

and his nostrils flared as if struggling to lift a herculean weight.

Felicity whirled around, aware that her bustle grazed his thighs.

Oh, lord. His thighs. Why did thinking of them make her blush?

Still immersed in the tragedy of her hem, Emmaline forged ahead. "Also, a curiously anxious Billings bade me to inform you that they're minutes from ringing the dinner gong— I haven't eaten a *thing* all day and am famished beyond all— oh, hello."

Finally, she glanced up to notice that they were not alone.

Felicity rushed to make introductions. "Emmaline, this is Mr. Gareth Severand, whom I've engaged as my personal protection. Mr. Severand, allow me to introduce Mrs. Emmaline Winterton, my chaperone and companion."

Emmaline's Baltic blue eyes went incredibly owlish as she looked up and up at the stoic Mr. Severand.

This must be the reaction he'd been expecting from Felicity.

Unease and suspicion mixed with curiosity.

Remembering her manners, Emmaline tore her eyes from his face and bobbed a curtsy. "A pleasure, Mr. Severand."

"Likewise," he rumbled from behind Felicity, sending shivers and stinging goose pimples thrilling over her flesh. His voice seemed quite two octaves lower than before. If that were possible. Was it because of Mrs. Winterton's radiance? Her shapely bared calf? Her heavy lashes and brilliant red hair?

Why should it matter if he found Emmaline pretty? She was pretty.

Emmaline retreated toward the door with backward

steps, as if she didn't want to turn her back on the mountainous man behind Felicity.

"Allow me to make myself presentable, and I'll harass the staff to make sure they set a place for Mr. Severand. Excuse me."

Felicity turned her chin to her shoulder, glancing behind her. "Shall we pour another drink and go through?" she offered, wary of being left alone with him at the moment. When all of her nerves zinged with a phenomenon both primal and electric.

His lashes shuttered his eyes as he looked away, but not before she caught the heat melting the metal of his gaze.

His tongue moistened a wickedly full lower lip before he answered, "After you."

CHAPTER 4

Back before Gabriel's surgeries, he was careful to never eat in the presence of anyone, not even his brother. The wounds to his cheek and the skin above his upper lip had healed so terribly that he could only open his mouth so far without ripping the scar open.

Since the skin grafts, he could eat with much more ease, but still hadn't much use for the behaviors and strictures of dining with the upper class.

He'd lived in a mansion not far from here for several odd years, but he took his meals alone in his chamber or in the library, and would have plucked the eyes out of anyone who dared disturb him.

How novel it was to use a dining room for its intended purpose. To appreciate centuries-old tapestries and priceless works of art illuminated by decorative lamps, crystal chandeliers no one bothered to light for such a small affair, and candelabras surrounded by fragrant garlands of fresh flowers.

Though he'd hesitated at the idea of sharing their meal, he found he enjoyed sitting at a long table across from the lively Mrs. Winterton as she chattered and exclaimed with Felicity over an abundance of swiftly altering subjects.

Their voices were a pleasant melody over the low hum of arousal vibrating through him, and while the women were distracted by their conversation, he could contemplate her.

He couldn't tell exactly what he'd expected when she'd drifted close to examine his features. Recognition, maybe? Or worse, fear. Disgust. Regret. Dismissal.

He'd been surprised— delighted, even— to receive none of that.

But when the air had shifted around them. When her pupils had dilated, and her lips parted as she stared at his own mouth...

He could have been knocked over with a feather.

Her proximity inflamed him as nothing else ever had, but surely he imagined that flare of interest behind the innocence of her gaze.

It was difficult to decipher, as she hadn't looked at him since.

When the soup course appeared in front of him, he plucked up what he knew to be the soup spoon, but didn't allow himself to partake until he could make a study of how the ladies conducted themselves.

He was, at least, clever enough to mimic their manners.

Across from him, Mrs. Winterton, now dressed in lilac silk, sans honey, dipped her spoon into her bowl and brought it to her lips, just so.

He dipped his own spoon in the same fashion, surreptitiously glancing over at Felicity, who frowned down into the liquid. She waited until the footmen had disappeared before wrinkling her nose. "Oh dear... Mrs. Bullock has made her fish stew."

Gabriel paused with a bite half to his mouth. "Is something wrong with it?"

"I cannot stomach it, I'm afraid." She pushed it away from her.

"Really?" Mrs. Winterton regarded her as if she were mad. "It's one of my favorite dishes. I mean, how could you hate anything that is half cream and salted with bacon?"

Felicity glanced around. "Here, have my portion," she offered to her companion.

"No, I have my own, and I'm not about to get on Cook's bad side."

"Quickly," Felicity pressed. "Before the footmen are back. Just pour it into your bowl. I don't want it getting to her that I didn't eat it, either. She's so proud of the dish. But last time, I could hardly keep it down."

"Very well. Quick, quick!" She slid her bowl closer to Felicity's and let her combine their portions before tucking into it with relish.

"What will you eat?" Gabriel queried, with a frown of his own.

"Oh, there's plenty of this fresh bread and a shank of braised lamb for the next course."

"And a rum pudding," said Mrs. Winterton after an appreciative swallow. "Do you enjoy the stew?"

He hated fish, but knew better than to say so. "I'll eat mostly anything," he answered, but returned the spoon to the bowl.

"I confess I'm glad you're here, Mr. Severand." Mrs. Winterton dabbed at the corner of her mouth. "We were all unspeakably distressed when poor Miss Felicity was accosted."

"We needn't speak of that," Felicity said tightly, fiddling with the black ribbon at her throat. "Now that Mr. Severand is here, we have little to concern ourselves with on that regard."

Before they dropped the conversation, he wanted to make one thing clear. "Miss Goode, I must insist you go nowhere without me, is that understood?"

"Are you in the habit of ordering all your employers

about?" Mrs. Winterton gave a saucy toss of her hair as she tightened the grip on her knife. "Or just the females? Let us not forget you are speaking to a baron's daughter."

"Emmaline, really!" Felicity's words conveyed less censure than mortification. Her cheeks were flaming the most adorable shade of peach. "I wasn't *planning* on going anywhere without him."

Winterton's eyes were… well… wintry as she glared over at him. "Yes, but he needn't be in the habit of issuing you commands. You are not the subordinate here."

Gabriel wiped his lips, slowly manufacturing a reply to the bold woman.

"You are right, of course, Mrs. Winterton."

At that, her mouth dropped all the way open. So he turned to Felicity.

"Forgive me, Miss Goode. I was not bred gently, and I am used to giving, rather than taking, directives. I do not possess pretty manners and am often too blunt in my speech. I will do my best to curtail this in your employ. My only aim is to keep you safe."

As he finished, he noticed that Felicity's eyes sparkled over at him like brilliant sapphires. Pleasure nigh glowed from her golden complexion.

"I did not engage you for pretty manners, Mr. Severand, but I do appreciate your respect. That being said, please speak freely in my presence; Lord knows I'm used to it with family like mine."

"Thank you."

He'd pleased her, and her satisfaction was a radiant sight to behold.

"Is everything all right with your family, Mrs. Winterton?" Felicity queried, slathering a soft cheese on a piece of bread and sinking her straight, pearly teeth into it.

Gabriel took a swallow of his excellent wine to wet a mouth gone dry.

Why did everything she did entice him so?

Why did the thought of her biting down on his flesh make him painfully hard beneath the table?

That was no great mystery…

"'Twas no great matter when all was said and done," Felicity's companion answered, seemingly preoccupied by her enjoyment of the soup. "It was almost a waste of time for me to visit. It seemed my younger sister had a spot of trouble, but she'd sorted it before I arrived. I only stayed long enough to kiss them all and catch the next train. It was frightfully tedious."

Gabriel noted that she'd never mentioned just what that trouble happened to be. Mrs. Winterton was a woman with an open, disarming face, and a heart better guarded than Buckingham Palace.

"I am sorry you are separated from your siblings." Felicity patted her arm. "I've always been lucky to have mine close by until… well, my parents' deaths changed a great deal, and now it seems we're scattered to the wind."

"Were you very close with your parents?" Gabriel ventured to ask.

She shook her head, rearranging the linen on her lap. "I was— am— the youngest in a disappointing line of girls. So, while they did their duty by me as their child, my parents were not wont to foster close relationships. Least of all with me."

"But your father left you everything." He blurted his thought aloud, then clamped his lips together, wishing he could rip his own tongue out.

She made a helpless gesture, as if the fact stymied her every bit as it did a stranger. "My father was first and foremost a businessman. Indeed, he was one of the few noblemen that noted the decline in landed estates early on. He used my mother's dowry to purchase a shipping company that he ruthlessly built into an empire. At first, the idle aristocracy jeered at and mocked him for becoming a tradesman. But then he became so obscenely wealthy, our family rubbed shoulders with the upper echelon of the *ton*, dining with earls and marquesses who were grudgingly glad to add my father to their ranks. Better one of their own than the upstart merchant men gaining social and political power these days."

Gabriel knew all this, of course; he'd used criminal means to exploit said shipping company for his smuggling enterprise a few years back. It was that decision that led him to where he sat today.

"Any idea why he left it all to you?"

She nodded. "He so much as said so in the amendment to his will. After Nora's disastrous marriage to a viscount, she ended up with an orphaned stable boy. Granted, Titus had become the most celebrated doctor in the empire, but that didn't matter to Father. A murder occurred at Pru's wedding, and she was first arrested for it, and then ended up wed to the chief inspector on the case. And then Mercy..." She sighed, glancing down at her lap. "There is not enough time for that story."

He did his best not to wince at the rueful note in her voice as she continued. "My father wrote that he'd always appreciated my sense of duty. That he believed me the last hope to save the face of the Goode name. He and my mother were so shattered by the scandals wrought by my sisters, he ran away from England. Nothing was quite the same after they left."

"You miss them?" He couldn't imagine why.

"I barely knew my mother, and I admired my father, but no, I do not miss his influence in my life. He was a hard man, critical and tempestuous, and his presence caused me no end of distress. He and my mother were devout in their faith. Zealots, some called them. He allowed us no joy or ease or freedom, and, if I'm honest, I've come to appreciate those things in his absence."

She blinked a little, her features arranging into a mask

of worry. "How terrible of me to speak of the dead thus. You must think me a monster."

He caught her gaze and held it. "I know monsters. You are not one."

Mrs. Winterton cleared her throat, and Felicity started, seeming to have forgotten her presence just as much as he had.

Schooling an uncomfortable look from her features, Emmaline visibly pushed a brightness into her eyes. "I did retrieve your gown and your haberdashery for tomorrow night," she said, making an obvious appeal for a change of subject. "It's as stunning as I thought it might be for your debut back into society."

"How kind of you, Emmaline." Felicity beamed a smile at her that had too many teeth.

"And Mr. Severand will be joining us?" Winterton lifted an eyebrow in his direction.

"He will."

"Do you dance, sir?" She tucked into her soup, sipping it whilst looking at him with rapt attention, as if more than vaguely interested in the answer.

"Not if I can help it."

She made a dismissive noise before turning back to Felicity. "Do not forget you have a stroll in the park with Lord Bainbridge before luncheon."

Felicity put a palm to her forehead. "Oh, that's right. I think he means to declare some intentions before the ball… I haven't any idea what to say."

Winterton's wide mouth shouldn't have been comely on anyone, but when she smirked like she did, with a twinkle of mischief in her eyes, Gabriel could appreciate how her features were arranged. They didn't touch the perfection of Felicity's, of course, but most men would find her handsome, he imagined.

"Let Bainbridge talk about himself," she advised with a bitter edge to her voice. "That's what men most prefer anyways. They'll think you have the most delightful personality so long as you have none at all."

Felicity gave an unladylike snort and a giggle, then tucked her lips together, casting him a conciliatory glance. "Forgive us, Mr. Severand, for maligning your sex. Emmaline is endlessly unkind."

Gabriel shrugged. "Unkind as it may be, Mrs. Winterton speaks the truth."

That earned him an approving look from the woman in question.

And a scowl from Felicity as she glanced from him to her companion.

Through most of dinner, Mrs. Winterton and Felicity spoke of schedules and events, of gossip and the garden. Gabriel didn't eat his stew, but found the lamb superb and the dessert uncommonly good. After the meal, his lids threatened to droop, his muscles untangled, and he found himself quite content to lounge at the table sipping his port until they'd quite finished their discussion.

He might not have many manners, but he knew to stand when the ladies did. He trailed them up the grand staircase and bade Mrs. Winterton good evening when she broke off to a second-floor bedroom. As a companion, she was another member of staff who didn't sleep with the servants.

He tried not to notice as Felicity stepped a couple of stairs above him, though her bustle was quite at eye level.

How strange that women changed their shapes thus.

What did Miss Felicity look like unclad? He'd seen her in her nightrobe, a billowy cream confection that left much to the imagination. And only then from a distance, backlit by a dim lamp through a window.

Christ, he was a mangled pervert. Good thing he wasn't staying. He couldn't look at her like this for long without going mad.

He trailed her down the third-story hall and was surprised when she stopped in front of his room, turning to address him. "Are your accommodations adequate, Mr. Severand?"

He loved the way the lamps gilded her hair like strands of spun gold. "More than adequate."

She seemed to cast about for something else to say.

"Since we'll spend so much time together, you might call me Gareth in private," he suggested. "If you like."

"I do like," she said brightly, then winced. "I mean, I'd be delighted. Might you call me Felicity? Or Miss Felicity, if you prefer."

"I might."

"Well..." She shifted, and he wondered if she was as reluctant to go as he was to let her. "I'm told I snore loud enough to be heard through the walls..." She trailed one fingertip across the blue arabesque paper. "So, I apologize if that disturbs you."

"It won't."

"Yes. That's good... I'll bid you goodnight then." She made no move to leave, merely traced the outline of the repeating pattern on the wall. He could watch her mind working, see the cogs and wheels turning while she searched for something to say.

"Is something troubling you?" he finally asked.

She looked up at him, suddenly appearing extraordinarily young. His fingers itched to smooth away the pinched lines of worry from her brow. "Nighttime is never extremely comfortable, is it? The dark is so full of silence and my thoughts are so terribly loud."

"I often find sleep infuriatingly elusive." He surprised himself by revealing something honest.

She bit her lip, then released it, transfixing him. "You know, I woke up dreading the day, but it turned out not to be so terrible after all."

"I'm glad of that."

"So... thank you, Mr.— erm— Gareth."

"Goodnight, Miss Felicity."

"Sweet dreams."

He watched her until she closed her door, knowing that if her voice followed him into his dreams, they'd be very sweet, indeed.

CHAPTER 5

Felicity thought Lord Duncan Murphy, the Earl of Bainbridge, was uncommonly handsome for a man just over forty. Vital and graceful and ceaselessly dashing, he did nothing without an effervescent flair, and could flay one alive with such cunning wit, most people forgave him instantly for making them laugh.

Ages ago, perhaps in a Tudor court, he'd have been a jester. Whispering satires into the King's ear and seductions beneath the queen's skirt.

Felicity did her utmost to pay attention to him as they strolled through Hyde Park.

The late morning held on to a pall of mist she and the tall, elegant rake on her arm displaced with their legs. The sun tried, and failed, to permeate the high clouds, but somehow the dew on the leaves still managed to linger and sparkle despite all that.

She did appreciate the tinge of silver threads teasing the auburn hair at his temples. And his whisky eyes glinted and snapped with his inescapable cleverness. He was uncommonly fit, and moved with an unaffected amble most would consider confident, but she thought bordered on the edge of arrogant.

Felicity catalogued these things as he spoke, having

lost the conversation some minutes prior. Following Mrs. Winterton's sage advice, she simply nodded and made encouraging noises when the tone or pitch of his voice seemed to warrant it.

So far, it'd worked like a charm.

It wasn't that she didn't enjoy Bainbridge's company, she did. Yet, her entire body— all her focus and awareness— was concentrated on the man following behind them at a circumspect distance.

Watching. Always watching.

Gareth Severand's gaze was a tangible thing, and she didn't find it at all unpleasant, merely distracting.

Upon awaking that morning, she'd rushed through her ablutions and toilette, more eager than usual to come down to breakfast.

Wrenching the door open, she'd frozen on the spot.

There, on a decorative table next to her door, sat a gleaming pair of spectacles and a watch hanging from a sapphire hummingbird brooch.

Someone had gone to the glasshouse in the night and found her missing treasures there. They'd cleaned them to a sparkling shine and returned them without disturbing her.

Without leaving a note or waiting until she was awake to deliver them into her hands and receive the deserved accolades.

She knew, without a doubt, that *he'd* done it.

Her servants were lovely, but they knew she preferred them to avoid the glasshouse. That was her domain. Her sanctuary. The one place she could go to truly be alone.

The thought of him lingering within the enclosure didn't at all bother her.

In fact, it—

"It is a happy thing to see you out of your dreadful mourning frocks, Felicity." Bainbridge sniffed his distaste. "You quite look like a sunbeam in that gown."

"Thank you," she murmured, smoothing her free hand over her velvet bodice. Everyone from Lucy, her lady's maid, to Mr. Bartholomew, to the driver of her carriage, commented on the loveliness of her new gown.

Everyone, that was, except Gareth Severand.

He'd merely scanned her once over from her hem to the feather in her cap. *Mutely* offered his hand to help her into the coach.

And then sat up with the driver.

Probably to keep a lookout for danger and all that...

His lack of notice didn't bother her. That would be silly. And it wasn't that she'd donned the frock with him in mind, per se.

But she *had* caught him admiring an amber-gold glass figurine the day before, and thought he might be partial to the color.

Now that she thought about it... perhaps he'd been admiring the shape of the nude woman the statue depicted, and not its shade at all.

"What color shall you wear to the ball tonight?" Bainbridge asked down at her. "I own every shade of buttonhole and tiepin, and should like to complement your gown."

"Oh, um... It's a gentle sort of color... not gold, not silver, not ivory... nor is it pink."

He let out a silken laugh that bared his even, white teeth. "Well, now that I know what it's *not,* I'm more intrigued than ever."

"It's a sort of diaphanous color, like champagne."

"And here you make a liar of me," he winked. "When I said I had every color, I forgot about champagne. I'll have to see what I can do on such short notice."

She cast him a conciliatory glance from beneath her lashes. "I'm sorry for being difficult."

"Think nothing of it." He nudged her affectionally.

"Speaking of difficult, you usually bring Mrs. Winterton along to these sorts of outings, do you not?"

Felicity winced in sympathy. "She is suffering the gastric effects of a poorly cooked fish stew."

His pout was meant to seem affected, but she thought there was some genuine disappointment in the gesture. "Poor thing. I was rather looking forward to her disapproving frown, icy glare, and scorching condemnation."

At that, Felicity smothered a giggle with her silk glove. "Oh, it's not so bad as all that. Mrs. Winterton barely approves of me. It's why she was hired, I think. Father liked nothing so much as a censorious person. And she's been ever so much kindlier since his passing."

"Yes, but I've often wondered why you keep her? Especially now that you have this strapping barbarian who's almost *half* as frightening as she is." He chuckled at his own joke.

Felicity had to be very careful not to check over her shoulder to ascertain if the strapping barbarian in question had taken offense.

"Mr. Severand is employed for my safety, not my companionship, and Mrs. Winterton reminds me of Mercy, so I can't help but like her very much. We're more friends than we are employer and staff."

"You have to be careful of that," he cautioned with a wry smile that didn't quite reach his eyes. "You let someone like that get close, and they'll take you for everything you have."

That drew her brows together. Bainbridge had always been a bit caustic, but she'd not known him to be so cynical.

"How many times should I dance at the ball with you?" he asked, levity returning to his manner as if he'd summoned it from thin air.

Felicity chewed on the inside of her lip, wondering if Bainbridge was every bit as wicked as he seemed, or much, much worse. She enjoyed his company always, but questioned if he was like this even when alone.

When no one was there to watch his spectacle.

"You know as well as I that dancing with me more than once would make a statement of intention..."

"And what do you think about that?" he pressed gently.

Her step faltered a bit, and she brushed it off as if checking her shoe for a flaw. "A statement? Are you implying you want to make one? But we're not... and you're..."

"Old?" His lips twisted into a rueful sort of smirk.

"I wasn't going to say that," she rushed to placate his feelings. "I mean, you are quite twenty years my elder, but I was more thinking about how a connection might come across as a bit... incestuous, you being my cousin and all."

"Second cousin," he corrected. "And I know that's fallen out of fashion these days, but we needn't even produce an heir if you're not inclined. I merely thought that since your father's title and certain lands passed to me upon his death, so, too, might your delightful self. Furthermore, you mentioned in the past, you'd like to find a way to keep the holdings together."

"I-I did, but..."

"Oh!" Bainbridge lifted a hand and waved enthusiastically at a group of gentlemen. "Pardon me, dear Felicity, I see a scoundrel with whom I must have a word. I'm going to leave you in the hands of this fellow for no longer than it takes for a kettle to whistle."

He hurried away over the green expanse of lawn, leaving her beneath the shade of a beech tree by a bench made of iron and oak.

Felicity sank onto it, unfocusing her eyes at her twirling her parasol as she fought a rising bout of nerves.

Bainbridge had spoken so blithely about marriage. As if it were a lark. But— God willing— she'd several decades to live her entire life. Deciding what that future would look like— and with whom she would share it—seemed like too monumental and overwhelming a task to leave in her own hands.

What if she made an enormous mistake? This was the sort of contract only broken by death.

Or worse, divorce.

She had no idea about marriage. Most of the books she read ended by the time the vows were spoken. And when asked, her sisters all claimed to have known the men they married were the loves of their lives. Their choices were absolute and their regrets nonexistent.

Whereas she... *she'd* received twelve proposals by post once she'd entered half mourning. Most of them from men she'd hardly met, and all of them little better than business contracts. Noblemen, politicians, even an impoverished duke, all offered to take over the running of her father's shipping company.

Indeed, her suitors thought that offering her a generous stipend of her own money was tantamount to courtship.

Bainbridge represented a different course, or so she thought. Someone she knew. Someone she liked.

However, behind his charm lurked something secretive, something that set alarm bells tolling in her head.

Was this fear valid, or something foisted upon her by her already nervous, overwrought disposition?

Blast, but it was bloody awful not to trust oneself.

She felt a presence before she heard the faint rustle in the grass beside the bench. A large body sheltered her from the increasingly chilly breeze as Gareth Severand stood sentinel at her side.

She glanced up at him, so glad to have the help of her spectacles to observe him.

Lord but he was compelling to look at. From every angle, she learned something new. Discovered a scar or mannerism she'd not previously detected. His teeth ground together when he pondered the world, as if chewing on his thoughts to make them more palatable. He'd a vein in his forehead, just beneath his widow's peak, that would appear when he was tense or irked. His eyes were never still, never fixed; they made ceaseless journeys across his entire vicinity, and she suspected he identified and catalogued any perceived threat, no matter how slight.

From this angle, she could tell he'd nicked himself shaving this morning beneath his jaw.

A vision of the man about his toilette distracted her from her troubled thoughts. His hair was combed back into organized layers tamed with pomade. His jaw clean-shaven, but threatened with a slight dark shadow in the places where the scars didn't shine.

She pictured him at the mirror, running a blade over his ruined cheeks, his hair in damp disarray and collar open, exposing his chest.

It was easier to picture him sprung from the darkness just as he was. Clean and dark and presentable. Never disheveled or rumpled.

Suddenly, her hand itched to glide through the strands of his tamed hair. To pull it and muss it and play among the glossy strands.

"Are you all right?" He never looked at her once, just stood by her side, scanning the promenading elite as if he expected to find an assassin in their midst.

Starting, she tore her gaze from appreciating him. "I find myself amazed, Mr.— er— Gareth." They were in public, but no one was paying them any mind. She felt alone enough to dare the intimacy of his first name. If she were honest, she needed the connection. "Does Bainbridge think that was some sort of proposal? To match his tiepin with my dress and dance with me more than once? What does a lady even do with that?"

That muscle ticked in his jaw as he rolled his shoulders in the semblance of a shrug.

Felicity craned her neck to look up at him until he finally seemed to feel her stare and glanced back.

A bemused wrinkle appeared between his brows, as if he were shocked that her question wasn't a rhetorical one. "I… wouldn't presume to imagine what a lady of your station might do in any given situation."

"How very politic of you." Her lips twisted in a rueful smile as she tried to hide her disappointment. It was not that she expected any sage advice from her personal guard, he was just the only person she knew in her vicinity at the moment.

"May I speak freely, Miss Felicity?"

"Only if you sit. I shall hurt my neck staring up at you." She scooted down the bench to make way for him, and he sank next to her, attempting a respectable distance.

The world really didn't make furniture large enough to accommodate men like him.

Their knees touched, and Felicity couldn't seem to move hers away.

If he noticed, he didn't make it obvious. Instead, he glared in the direction of Bainbridge and his cadre of gentlemen, maybe six in all, who were hanging upon his every word. "Is there a chance this Bainbridge has ulterior motives?" he ventured with apparent caution.

"Such as?"

"How would a match with you benefit him?"

At this question, she frowned. "I don't know; he did inherit my father's title of Baron, but he tucks it under his own far greater one of Earl. He's possessed of vast estates and a good name. I can only think he's offering out of a sense of kindness or duty."

His stony features shifted only in barely perceptible increments from grim to dire.

"You don't agree?" she assessed.

"I don't trust kindness and duty as motivations for anyone, especially men like Bainbridge." He flicked his gaze to her, squinted, and looked back at Bainbridge as if his eyes couldn't land upon her for too long.

"In your professional experience, how does one go about assessing another's motivations?" she puzzled.

"You could try asking him."

At his dry suggestion, Felicity made a sound of consternation in the back of her throat before she drew back to take in his entire expression.

A muscle in his cheek tightened, lifted, and his grey eyes glinted with something more soft than sharp.

He was teasing her.

"Don't be a cad," she admonished with a smile, before following his gaze to her cousin. He was a rather stunning individual. All lithe and lovely in a bespoke grey suit. His skin perfect, his jaw angular, and his teeth astonishingly straight. Half the women in Christendom wanted Bainbridge as their lover. The other half had reportedly had him already.

She blew her cheeks out on an eternal sigh. "I hate asking uncomfortable questions more than just about anything in the world. I'm always afraid people will be hostile or humiliating. Especially someone like Bainbridge, with his famously sharp wit."

"I'll not tolerate so much as an unkind word." As was his way, the declaration was spoken in low matter-of-fact tones, but his eyes were as cold and hard as tempered steel.

Felicity had to swallow twice before she replied. "I… I am glad of your company today, Gareth. I think you've helped me a great deal."

His gaze flicked down, spearing the grass between his feet. His hands laced together across his knees with a white-knuckled grip.

"The morning was so chaotic with Mrs. Winterton's illness and all, I didn't have the chance to thank you for finding my spectacles and watch," she persisted.

"Was nothing," he mumbled at the ground.

"It wasn't nothing to me." She laid her hand over his forearm to emphasize her point. "If they are lost, so am I. I hate not being able to see, but the lenses get so foggy in the glasshouse. You quite saved me from being blind for days whilst waiting on the optician. And this watch is a treasured gift from Mercy." With her free hand, she fondled the brooch above her breast.

He brushed her words off with a shrug, but a crimson stain crept above his collar and spread across his entire face until his very ears tipped with it.

A man like Gareth Severand *blushed*? Had there ever been anything more endearing on this entire earth?

He grunted and shifted in his seat, pulling his arm from her grip. "Your suitor/cousin is returning." He thrust his chin in that direction.

The bite in his voice really did make a blood connection with Bainbridge sound like some sort of perversion.

"He's a distant cousin," she found herself defending.

He merely made an indecipherable noise in the back of his throat.

Felicity stood, creating space between herself and Gareth. That distance felt cold. Something like abandonment.

How very odd.

"I do appreciate your patience, darling." Bainbridge tucked her hand back into the crook of his arm and continued their stroll.

"Duncan?" Felicity's heart kicked against her ribs and her stomach rolled, so she focused on the sound of the crunch beneath the heavy boots of the man behind them.

"Yes?"

"Do you *want* to marry me?"

He threw his head back and laughed merrily for so long, she wondered if she should take offense. "Generally, the proposal is the gentleman's purview, but I *do* appreciate a lady with initiative." He gave a few more chuckles. "You astonish me, Felicity Goode, as I thought you were more of a mouse than that. All right. You've talked me into it. I'll marry you."

She thought she heard a groan from behind her, which helped not at all.

Pressing her gloves to heated cheeks, she amended, "I wasn't proposing. I mean— I thought you'd already... that is... I was asking if you desired the match. Or rather, *why* you desired it. If you do— that is. Desire it."

He regarded her as if she'd grown horns and a tail.

She began to babble like a brook swelled in spring, overflowing the banks and spilling over. "I'm asking, I suppose, *why* you want to marry. More specifically, why you'd want to marry *me*. I do not know what I have to offer you of interest... Do you want children?" Was that it? Was he interested because of her youth?

This time, his laughter was shorter, tinged with a note of uneasiness. "I mean, I'm not opposed to children, if you insist. I'm almost certain I have a brat or two running around."

She took in a sharp breath. Had he *really* just admitted that whilst discussing marriage with her?

He stopped in their tracks, turning to her and taking both her gloved hands in his own. "I'm sorry, darling, I'm endlessly wicked. How would you ever stand me?"

She didn't know that she wanted to.

"Do you think you could love me?" she breathed.

His face softened and he brought the knuckles of each hand in for a kiss. "I already adore you, Felicity, you know that."

She tightened her grip on his fingers, making his smile

disappear. "I mean *love* me, Duncan? Truly? Affectionately… faithfully?"

He cleared his throat and surreptitiously looked around at the shimmering gaiety of the parading *ton*. Sincerity didn't sit on his features with ease, but Felicity was certain this was the first time she was about to hear the truth pass his lips. "Felicity, an arrangement between us would be of mutual fondness and respect. I'd make you a countess, and upon our marriage, your father's holdings would belong to me. If I'm honest, without them, I'll be forced to sell off some land to keep up my estates."

"You want me for the money?" She pulled her hands away.

"I'll admit that's part of it. But… due to recent events, I find myself in need of a wife, and I already enjoy you so much, I think we'd suit. You'd be free to live as you like. Take a lover or two. Travel the Continent. Et cetera. But I won't lie to you and say that I won't do the same. I know you were raised innocent by your tyrannical father, but it is the way of our class. We could get on, you and I?"

"I…" Felicity couldn't think of a single word to say.

"I've distressed you," he pouted. "I apologize, my dear."

The apology sounded genuine, and Felicity found herself swallowing irritation, understanding, gratitude, and a myriad of other confounding emotions. "I merely… need some time to consider things, I suppose."

"Of course." He made a gesture of benevolence. "Here. We'll dance tonight all of once, so no one makes any assumptions about us. I'm not in dire straits, darling, and I've plenty of heiresses to pick from should you not think we'll get on. Either way, we should always remain friends and cousins." He was all earnest eyes and candid charm.

"Of course. Always. Thank you for your honesty, Duncan. I *am* very fond of you. I think I shall return home now to prepare for this evening."

"I look forward to our waltz." He kissed her hand once

more before bowing over it, something dark and melancholy passing over his features.

Suddenly, Felicity wanted to cry.

"Good afternoon." She turned around and swept back through the park, keeping a firm tamp on her emotion until she was certain no one was watching.

"I'm not going to marry him," she stated rigidly to her giant, silent shadow.

"Good," came the clipped reply.

"I cannot be the only one of my sisters without fidelity. I am not built for that. I'd be miserable."

"Bainbridge surprised me," he remarked, surprising her in turn. "Not many men are so frank. Which makes me think he is either a good man, or he has a secret deeper than his apparent wickedness to hide. Something ruinous. Something lethal even."

"Do you think so?"

"I'd bet my fortune on it."

That gave her something to wonder over until the dreaded ball. "Well... Let's do go home, Gareth, I need to bathe and—"

The man beside her tripped on absolutely nothing. With impressive reflexes and an extra step, he was able to prevent a fall or even much of a spectacle.

"Bloody rocks," he muttered.

She said nothing, not wishing to embarrass him. Though her conversation with Bainbridge was troubling, she felt a bit lighter than before. How fortunate she was that Gareth had been here today, prompting her to ask the correct questions.

What a boon to have a forthright and honest man at her side. Looking out for her. Listening to her troubles. Offering support and wisdom. Giving her the confidence to act on her own.

Wouldn't it be wonderful to have that always?

CHAPTER 6

Gabriel had assumed that once he was rid of his mask, he'd never wish to lay eyes upon it again.

It troubled him how much he wanted it now.

Even dressed in an impeccable evening suit, he could never hope to blend in.

Which meant he stood out, especially amongst the *ton*.

It was known he was a servant, of a sort, but not one that could be kept busy and invisible, such as a footman or a maid. His job was to watch, and his gaze made people mindful of their behavior.

Exactly no one appreciated that feeling.

While some regarded him with caution, hostility, disgust, or outright fear, he found that easy to ignore. What puzzled him the most was the reactions of several women to his presence.

Curiosity.

He leaned against a wall adjacent to a sideboard laden with largely untouched canapés, doing his best to disappear into the wallpaper. He'd noted that many of the women in the grand ballroom seemed to fabricate reasons other than food to gracefully flit by him like a cadre of vibrant butterflies.

In fact, he'd retrieved more than a half dozen accidentally discarded handkerchiefs from the floor in front of him. Had held multiple drinks as one lady or other fixed a bunched hem or broken lace behind the fern to his left, exposing varying lengths of their ankles and calves. A matronly marchioness had quite lost her balance and fell into his arms in an apparent swoon. She'd somehow made it impossible to avoid the press of her abundant bosoms as he righted her, and had promised him her generous gratitude if he called upon her tomorrow after her husband had gone to the House of Lords.

Indeed, more than a handful of married ladies did their utmost to convince their husbands that they were in need of his *particular* personal protection just as much as any orphaned, bookish baron's daughter. One of them had overtly gestured to his features and proportions as a deterrent from a husband's jealousy. What would he have to worry about around such an ungainly brute?

Unsurprisingly, he received no offers of employment from any man in the room.

Not only did the attention make him feel freakish and uncomfortable, but it also made his job more difficult than it ought to be.

Felicity was the only woman who deserved his attention tonight. All others were nothing more than an irritation.

An irritation that was swiftly compounding by the stifling heat and closeness of the ballroom, the fiendishly relentless music, and the sheer number of men who'd held Felicity Goode in their arms that evening.

In Gabriel's imagination, he'd already broken seven arms and gouged out numerous eyes.

This was hell.

Lucifer himself was taking his due earlier than expected, by making him watch her smile up at elegant and well-mannered men of her class.

And wondering if he would be the man to win her.

As promised, she and Lord Bainbridge had shared a sedate dance, and the man had been nothing but solicitous and polite.

He'd relinquished her company to a squat, red-faced hedgehog of a man upon whom she bestowed a benevolent smile, and even struck up a lively chat.

All the while, others laughed behind their gloves and their fans.

At her. At her partner.

Several lordlings lingered around the food, gazing at her like wolves circling a wide-eyed fawn. They grinned their sharp-toothed grins as they guessed who would next come up on her card. They bragged about saving her from having to kiss a toad like Lord Kessinger. About dazzling her with their pedigrees and their family estates.

All the while, Gabriel yearned to tear them all open. Sternum to throat.

He stood at the ready, waiting for them to give him a reason.

Just one.

After an eternity, the waltz ended, and the benighted Mr. Kessinger escorted her from the dance floor, looking for all the world as if he'd gained two inches in height.

Gabriel knew how the man felt.

A smile from her was akin to a kiss from the sun or God's very own forgiveness.

And tonight, she was every inch a goddess.

Champagne silk threaded with some sort of glimmering magic was certainly not secured upon her body by the hoaxes they had the nerve to call sleeves. Gauzy fabric with the substance of a whisper draped from her shoulders, leaving her flesh all but bare from her jaw to the edge of the ivory gloves that crested above her elbow.

Her bodice, if one could call it that, revealed more than it covered, as various contraptions beneath foisted her breasts higher than they had any right to be. Offering up each delectable mound like an apple of Eve, tempting any unsuspecting man to have a taste. The skirt, while not tight or formfitting, gave the illusion of clinging to her hips in what he'd gleaned from ladies' gossip, was the new— and some said, *indecent*—fashion.

He couldn't disagree. When she walked, the outline of her thighs appeared beneath the skirts, before the flowing fabric belled out to swirl around her knees and feet like a gossamer mist.

When Gabriel had removed her cape upon their arrival, it'd taken all his willpower not to wrap her back up in it, toss her over his shoulder, and conduct her out of the sight of anyone.

Anyone, but himself.

As she approached, Gabriel noted that beneath her tranquil demeanor were the barest hints of strain. A small pinch between her brow, a whitening at the corner of her lips, and a shadow beneath her eyes that contrasted with skin three shades paler than usual.

Even so, she turned to Lord Kessinger, who ignored Gabriel, and sank into a graceful curtsy. "Thank you for a most enjoyable dance, my lord," she proffered, enduring the kiss he hovered above her knuckles before retreating to Gabriel's side.

With a grateful, if brittle, smile, she accepted the glass of punch Gabriel had procured for her, and stifled a yawn behind her glove.

"You should drink," he prompted when, instead of sipping the punch, she surveyed the ballroom much as he had been doing the entire night.

"What?" she asked distractedly.

He gestured to her cup. "You'll overheat if you don't drink."

"Oh, how thoughtful of you." She took several long sips from the crystal glass, pressing a glove to a sheen at her hairline. "What do you think of Lord Kessinger, Mr. Severand?"

Now that they were in public, he was Mr. Severand once more.

"I *don't* think of him."

She gave a wry smile from behind the lip of her glass. "You're being cheeky," she accused.

Affronted, he lifted his chin. "I've never been cheeky in my life."

A soft sound of amusement escaped her. "That, I do believe of you. But, pray tell me, what is your impression of him?"

He hadn't meant to amuse her. In fact, it irked him that he had. "Why do you ask my opinion? *I'm* not the one contemplating marriage."

"I ask because you read people, I think. Like I read books. You predict their motivations. Like with Bainbridge, for example, you knew what a scallywag he was before he admitted it himself."

Her praise did serve as a *slight* balm to his foul temper. "Scallywag?" he echoed, tugging at his noose of a necktie.

"Isn't that a delicious word?" she breathed. "I finished *The Gilded Sea*, but because of it I am now obsessed with buccaneers and privateers, so I'm reading about this monstrous pirate king who is often called things like *scallywag, picaroon,* or *coxswain.*"

He bit his lip, vowing to forget that last word from her lips.

"Another romantic adventure?" he posited.

"Yes, except this time, he falls for a mermaid."

His lip curled of its own volition. "Sounds…"

"Fantastical and exciting?" she offered.

"I was going to say fragrant," he muttered. "I'm no great lover of fish."

She tilted her head back and laughed, a sound of mild yet unbridled mirth.

The world stood still to hear it.

"I was wondering why you barely touched your stew last night," she teased. "Cook must be so offended."

"Not as offended as my nose."

"Stop, you." She nudged him with another chuckle, indulging in more punch. "Well, *there* is something we have in common, as I am no great lover of fish, either. I have, however, reassessed my opinion on scallywags. I find this pirate king so very compelling. He's all scarred and heavily tattooed and he says the most wicked things. I'm surprised they allow it in the bookshops."

Gabriel's mouth flooded as he considered what wicked words might put such a rapturous look upon her face. "Pirates make notoriously terrible husbands," he reminded her.

As did smugglers, he reminded himself.

"Well, certainly, if we're being practical. But he is a man with a creed and a big heart. Besides, he redeems himself in the end."

He slanted a dubious look down at her. "You can't know that; you're not done with the book."

"All romances end like that."

"Why read them if you know the ending?"

She turned to look up at him, her expression both playful and profound. "Because one likes to watch the journey unfold. We all know how *life* ends, don't we? But we don't live it to hurry toward death. It's the matter in the middle that's the most important. Besides, I know romance might not be the most respected subject, but there are times when one needs to know that at least in one story, everything ends as it should… happily."

Humbled by such wisdom wrapped in a package of guileless youth, Gabriel could only gape at her for a protracted moment.

"Don't marry Kessinger." The words spilled from his mouth before he could call them back.

"Why would you say that?" Her eyes searched his, a strange, liquid hope in their azure depths.

"He's not... well, just look at him." He turned to where the man had taken up a card game in the next room over. The odious man blew his nose at that unfortunate moment, then looked into the handkerchief before stowing it away.

They each winced.

"He can't help how he looks," she defended the man, though her fingers were pressed to her throat in a gesture of aversion. "And it's not so bad as all that. I thought he had kind eyes, and we shared the most diverting conversation. He's a true gentleman, they say. No vices or villainy. He's studious and methodical and I found him indulgent and interesting."

"Be that as it may, a woman as handsome as you should take a handsome husband."

Her lashes swept down over cheeks tinged with peach. "You think I'm handsome?"

"Don't be coy," he said with a droll sniff.

"No one has ever called me coy before," she informed him, turning back to study Kessinger. "Handsome isn't so important to me in a husband. Not if he is good and gentle and kind."

Good, gentle, and kind. That was all she required, and he still didn't fit the bill. Something dark and wretched twisted in his chest. "Don't you see it would be heartless to select him? People would speculate. They would be cruel to him, insinuate you were with him for any of the ugly reasons people marry for. Desperation. Power. Titles. Indulgences. They'd expect you to cuckold him. They'd count the months in between your wedding and an heir and speculate as to whom the child belongs."

Aghast, she lifted a hand to her lips. "You don't really think—"

"He would resent you, in the end."

The shadows in her eyes became bruises as she contemplated this, then the liquid blue hardened to chips of ice as she scowled up at him. "How would you know anything about it? Someone with your attractions, your masculine allure, could never hope to empathize with poor Mr. Kessinger."

"*Now* who is being cruel?" he sneered.

"What?" Her glare gave way to several confounded blinks. "How might a compliment be cruel?"

"When it is so blatantly for the sake of kindness," he pointed out the bloody obvious. "Such as calling a portly person thin, or someone like me attractive."

"But—"

"Miss Goode, I believe I am next on your card." One of the wolves, a fair-haired fellow blessed with almost symmetrical perfection, sidled up to her with a gallant hand outreached in offering.

Fumbling a bit, Felicity checked the card on her wrist. "So you are, Lord Melton." She slid her hand into his and allowed him to lead her to the floor, only frowning back at Gabriel the once.

His blood heated to a degree that could surely smelt metal. Sweat bloomed on his flesh just as a dull, cold pit developed in his chest.

Masculine allure.

Was that what sent handkerchiefs fluttering to his feet, and jaded, middle-aged women swooning into his arms?

Posh birds love a bit of rough, Raphael had once said to him on his way to a night of debauchery.

His eyes devoured Felicity as she seemed to melt into Lord Melton's arms.

Would she?

Not bloody likely. Gabriel wasn't *a bit of rough,* he was an entire mountain of it. His hands, his body, his heart, his vocabulary and comportment.

His need.

This was fucking torture.

The sight of Melton's hand on the curve of her back. His arms directing her this way and that as they floated over the dance floor. Their bodies a whisper away from each other, her skirt comingling with his legs.

That should be me.

The thought clawed its way through his head, and he grappled the beast back into its cage.

No. It should not.

What sort of offer could he make a woman like her? What did he have *to* offer her? His past and his sins and the blood on his hands? The money he'd amassed by pilfering from her fellow nobles, or doing their dirty work?

Enemies that would seek to crush her. That might already be trying to do so.

A life of secrets and darkness?

No, she needed to be here in the light, waltzing beneath crystal chandeliers doing their utmost to match her innate illumination. She was a creature meant for this glittering place and these gentle lads.

And he could only hope to watch her from the shadows.

Gabriel couldn't take much more of this. He needed to find out who posited a threat to her, kill them most brutally, and take to the wind once she was safe.

Before she could uncover his deception.

Perhaps she *should* marry Kessinger. The hedgehog *was* a gentle-looking man. He'd at least keep her on the pedestal she deserved.

Images of the viscount rutting on top of her made him turn to the table beside which he stood. He came within an inch of flipping the entire thing over, just to watch everything shatter and everyone scream.

Thinking better of it, Gabriel escaped to a small private garden whose doors had been flung open to air out the increasingly warm ball room, but the entry had been roped off to deter guests.

He burst into the cool, familiar night, gulping in lungsful of the cool evening air.

Fuck. Fuck. Fuck. He needed to break something.

Someone.

He didn't belong here. Not in this world. He wasn't worthy to touch the silk hem of her gown.

Plunging his fingers through his hair, he gave a frustrated tug. What was he doing? What had he been thinking? How had he allowed himself to be pulled into this strange world wherein he slept beneath her roof and followed her around like some protective overgrown puppy?

All because he'd pathetically craved her presence for so long. Yearned to speak to her. To touch her. To be a part of the world in which she lived, and was presented with the inexplicable opportunity to do so.

He should have known this would be a disaster. He wanted all the eyes that touched her to be gone, to keep her only for himself like some primitive savage.

He'd vowed that once he'd dismantled his father's organization, he'd no longer be a beast. That his only revenge could be to refuse the legacy intended for him.

But here he was, wanting to rip a man apart with his teeth. To truss up a woman— with or without her permission— carry her back to his den and…

And…

And what? He'd never be able to degrade such an angel with the wicked— fiendish— acts his body yearned for.

And he'd no experience with the act. No skill or reference.

Just unspent lust and unfulfilled need.

A prickling of his skin alerted him to an interloper silently approaching from behind.

Gabriel's hand reached beneath his jacket to find the

blade secured to his back before turning to face the very subject of his tormented reflections.

"It's unbearably hot in there." Felicity feathered a glove over her flushed brow. "What a splendid idea to escape."

He shook his head, pointing to the door. "You should go back inside. It won't do to be caught out here together. If you're overheated, we can take refuge in the public gardens—"

"I can't face the public gardens." She frantically looked about, finding a hedge to the side of the door that blocked a cozy pergola from view. Retreating to it, she sank to a bench and bent forward as far as her corset would allow, breathing heavily, her face pinched with tension.

Struck with concern, Gabriel went to her. "Are you unwell? Do you think whatever is plaguing Mrs. Winterton has found you?"

She shook her head, still visibly fighting for breath.

"Then what is it?" He hovered over her, his hands itching to examine her, but for what, he couldn't begin to define. "Should we take you to Dr. Conleith?"

His ruse would be over, but that didn't matter if she were in danger.

Again, she gestured in the negative, holding up a hand for his silence as she fought some internal battle he could only watch.

Finally, after a minute or two, she dropped her forehead into her hands and let out an eternal breath. "It's over... It wasn't as dreadful as it can be." The words muffled against her gloves.

He sank beside her, his heart, already galloping with his own turmoil, now racing with concern for her. "What is over? What is wrong?"

The eyes that met his were so haunted he could barely stand it. "Do you ever feel like you're empty, Gareth? Like you've run out of words and wit and energy? Like your smile is so heavy and yet so brittle, the muscles can no longer keep it aloft? And all this because people took that smile from you... demanded it from you, even when it seems you have less to give than most?"

The bleak note in her voice stole his ability to speak.

The side of her mouth quirked at him. "Of course not. You don't smile in the first place. And no one dares to command you."

She could.

He tried on a smile for her. It had been so long, but he made the valiant effort. Wrinkled his eyes and relaxed his lips into a soft curl.

"Look at that, it does exist." Her gloved fingers lifted, as if she thought to touch his mouth, to test his attempt with her fingers.

Ultimately, she thought better of it.

"You are pale," he pressed. "Are you certain you're not ill?"

"No, I just... I have spells sometimes." She frowned down at her fingers in her lap, curling them tightly. "When I'm overwhelmed or upset."

At that, he became instantly alert. He never should have come out here. Shouldn't have left her side for a moment, thinking her safe in a sea of her peers, dancing in a crowded room.

"Who upset you?" he demanded.

She lifted a creamy shoulder. "No one. *Everyone.* I-I just... I don't have anything to say to these people. And, if I'm honest, I don't want to hear what they have to talk about either. I don't care about gossip or politics, fashion or scandal. And they don't care about botany or books. They all hate each other and yearn to impress each other in this perverse and endless circle of deceit, envy, and need."

Looking up, she closed her eyes and let the breeze toy with the wisping ringlets at her temples and neck. "I'm being overly harsh, I know. I have to learn to belong here.

Or everything I have is gone… And yet, even if I do select this life, everything I have goes to whomever I chose to marry." She opened her eyes and stared up into the vast canopy above them as if she could find answers there. "I am inconsequential either way… Sometimes I really do wish I were born a man. Though I would have made a terrible one."

Gabriel ached to pull her close. Her circumstance did induce a well of sympathy he'd not previously had. How could someone be so privileged and helpless all at once? Was there a way out of this?

"You could untether from your fortune," he suggested. "Turn to any one of your family members and be done with all of this." He waved his arm toward the ballroom, where the orchestra was tuning for another waltz.

She chewed on her lip. "I know this is going to sound strange, but now that my father's company is in my hands, I feel so utterly responsible for it. When I select someone to marry, I am selecting a future not only for me, but for the business. For the country.

"My father's industry employs so many people. The vessels bring food, mechanical imports, implements of everything from medicine to textiles. It's such a worthy endeavor, shipping. Such an important part of the economy and society. I'm loath to abandon that to just anyone. And…"

She pushed away from the bench, pacing the length of the pergola with her arms crossed tightly over her chest. "When it comes to my family… I'd thought to grow old with Mercy, but now…" She turned to grasp the railing and stare up at the half moon. "Do you want to know my greatest fear? Being the spinster sister in the corner watching everyone in love. I want to belong somewhere. To someone."

"Someone like Melton?" Gabriel ventured, remembering how she'd looked in the man's arms.

She astonished him by laughing. "Least of all Melton. He was vapid and smelled like he'd bathed in aftershave. I can still taste it." She made a face.

His wry sound of amusement seemed to distress her, and her pacing quickened, her gestures becoming animated.

"I know I'm being selective. But I *want* what is in the novels. I want to be struck by lightning and shaken by thunder. I want to put my heart in a man's hands and know he'll keep it safe. I couldn't abide a useless lord who would while away my fortune as I sat and watched and withered into a bitter old woman. Is it too much to ask to not only share love with a man, but admiration and respect, as well? To find someone who makes this world better for being in it? Sometimes I feel like I'm this endless abyss of unfulfilled desire and I— I can never ask for what I need. I can never find it. I don't have the courage."

She flopped against one of the columns, resting her head against it with aggrieved antipathy. "And so here I am. Hiding in the garden like I always do."

A hollow ache lodged within as he watched her bare her heart to the night.

He knew the longing she felt, acutely.

Except, he'd already found the lightning, it struck him breathless each time he saw her.

He wished to be the answering thunder.

But he was nothing like the man she'd described. Feeling raw and exhausted and more than a little bleak, he drifted to the pergola steps, putting space between them.

"I… take it you're done dancing for the evening, then?" he said hopefully. "Should I call for the carriage?"

She nodded, casting a longing glance back toward the ballroom. "If I had my druthers, I'd dance until my legs gave out. I love it so much, losing myself to the rhythm, focusing only on the music and what my feet are doing… It's the only time my thoughts are truly quiet. Usually, I'm Nora and Mercy's bespectacled little sister. No one of consequence. But tonight, I could feel everyone watching and I… I forget how to dance." She pushed a breath through her lips, puffing them out. "There are days I hate who I am." Her little fists clenched, and she shook with an emotion other than fear. He watched the war on her features with a helpless compassion.

Without thinking, he stood and went to her, offering his hand. "No one is watching now."

She blinked up at him in confusion. "You said you didn't dance."

"I know the basics, I suppose." He lifted a shoulder. "You can lead. I'll follow. I'm a quick study."

"Me lead?" She looked around the private garden as if he'd said something scandalous. "You won't feel… I don't know… emasculated?"

At that a true smile touched his lips, one he couldn't suppress if he wanted to. "Miss Felicity, if my manhood could be threatened by learning something from a woman, then I wasn't much of a man to begin with."

His words seemed to please her so much, she unclenched her fingers before sliding her glove into his. "Indeed not." The smile she granted him had lost its brittle edge.

She stood across from him, glittering like a moonbeam, and set her hand on his shoulder, moving into the circle of his arms. Her fingers disappeared into his as she stretched their hands away from their bodies to adopt the waltzing posture.

Gabriel stood still and solid, worrying that she'd change her mind. That somehow, she'd recognize him.

He knew it was gauche to look at her, that their necks should arch away to avoid the intimacy of eye contact.

But she never broke her gaze from his as she stepped

one way, and then— encouraged by his effortless follow— she stepped again. And again.

Gabriel's body attuned to her every gentle cue, to the nearly imperceptible nudges of her hands. The soft wisp of her slippers as they kissed his shoes, urging him in time to the music. This waltz was a slow one, thankfully giving him time to adjust. He'd watched her dance once before at the disastrous Midnight Masquerade and marveled at the change in her. The confidence she'd possessed when she'd drifted out of her mind and into her body.

Just as she did now.

The temptation to join her in that place was undeniable, and before long, Gabriel became lost in the rhythm of their movement and her breath and his thrumming heart.

"You, Gareth Severand, are either a liar or a natural," she said after a while, her eyes twinkling in the dim light of the garden lanterns. "I can hardly believe you've not done this before."

"A liar," he confessed ruefully. "My mother did teach me a bit before she died."

"Oh?"

A pang lanced his heart at the memory. His lovely, young, ebony-haired mother trying to teach an impatient boy of eight a new waltz. "That was very long ago. I hardly thought to remember."

"It sounds like the memories of your mother are good ones."

"All of them," he murmured.

"And your father?"

The last thing he wanted in this conversation, in this moment with this woman so close to his body, was the intrusion of his father.

"None of them."

Observant as she was, she seemed to accept discussion on that account was closed.

They were silent a moment, lost in the steps. In their thoughts.

"Do you really not have a sweetheart?" she ventured. "I think that's an awful shame."

Lord, but did she think to poke every bruise his soul possessed?

"No. I do not."

"Why not?" Her mouth drew into a vague little pout. "Did someone break your heart?"

No, but she would eventually.

"My heart is not sweet, Miss Goode," was all he could offer by way of explanation.

"I don't believe that."

"You don't know who I am."

She considered that for a moment, narrowing her eyes in thought. "Who are you, then?"

Gabriel swallowed over a gathering lump in his throat.

He could tell her.

I'm the man who took a bullet for you. He could say. *I'm a gangster used to wielding power and precedence over an organization of ruthless criminals. I am a damned soul who has done unspeakable things to survive. My brother is married to your sister and I've been watching you for longer than Raphael even knew the two of you existed.*

Who am I? I am Gabriel Sauvageau. The fallen prince of a dismantled empire.

And I love you.

He said none of that as he gazed down at her upturned face. He was too selfish a bastard to utter anything that might drive her from his arms.

He loved her.

He wasn't certain how to describe the phenomenon before now.

But he loved her. He did. He thought about her every morning upon waking. Every night before sleeping. He pictured her when pleasuring himself. He'd kept her image on the backs of his eyelids during the months of suffering through the several surgical procedures that left him only just palatable to be seen in public without a mask. Her safety and comfort were his first priority, a responsibility he assigned to himself without a thought of asking for anything in return.

"It doesn't matter who I am," he whispered, distracted by the light gilding the soft moisture on her lips with an ethereal sheen. "Not tonight."

All the reasons he shouldn't touch her disappeared into the darkness, fleeing before the creature of primitive instinct the moon and the music seemed to make of him.

His blood roared. His cock filled. His muscles tensed and built into a straining, pulsing machine, overwhelmed with the need to find other, more primal rhythms.

But he would rip out his own heart before he succumbed to any of that.

Because the soft cling of her fingertips against his shoulder was enough to keep the entire monster leashed with unbreakable chains.

Everything that was hard and horrible about himself, rough and possessive, selfish and violent, he beat back with all the considerable strength he possessed.

Which left him powerless to resist her.

Only when her hand left his grasp to rest against his jaw, did he notice that they'd stopped moving. That her mouth had parted, and his shoulders had already curled forward.

His head lowered.

Her toes lifted.

The breath that feathered across his face was warm and vaguely flavored of fruit from the punch. Her intricate coiffure gleamed like gilded braids of gold and he imagined her skin was as smooth as cream whipped to a froth.

But it was the way her lids became heavy across eyes darkened with the very same need roaring through him, that unraveled the last of his sanity.

The invitation he read there.

His mouth hovered above hers for the last futile moment, if only to give her a chance to pull away. To deny him. To retreat.

Because once he tasted her, he wasn't certain when he'd be able to stop.

Her response suffused him with absolute shock.

She placed the shortest, gentlest, *barest* of kisses on his lower lip. One little, encouraging sweep accompanied by the scarcely audible click of her mouth puckering and releasing.

It was all he needed to seal his lips to hers.

Gabriel had always known that Felicity Goode was crafted of equal parts warmth and softness. But he could have never imagined what those seemingly innocuous words even meant until this moment.

With a sibilant sigh, her lips pillowed his with an excruciatingly sweet welcome.

Within the very structure of him, parts softened and weakened, threatening to give way beneath the onslaught of hunger ravaging him from the inside out.

Other parts— one other part in particular— became so instantly rock-hard, he moaned at the glorious ache of it.

He did not crush her to him as he yearned to do, not when his every instinct screamed at him to find a way to meld with her. To crawl inside her warmth and stay there, until the cold world forgot he ever existed.

Instead, he cautiously cupped her face in his hands, mindful of the delicacy of her bones, holding her as if she were made of spun sugar.

For surely, she must be to taste so unbearably sweet.

The kiss didn't remain frozen or still. Their lips moved without skill or haste, even as tendrils of disquieting emotion unfurled through him like ribbons of quicksilver, settling into the sinew of his muscle and meat.

With this one small press of flesh, this melding of mouths and breath, Felicity Goode claimed him as her own.

There was no woman before her, and he could imagine no one after. He'd looked upon others with desire plenty in his life, but never with the hope to have them. Never with the instantaneous pull she'd had over him from the very first time they'd met.

She'd been standing right next to her twin, a mirror image in beauty and bearing.

But just as she'd described, he'd been struck as if by lightning, and somehow knew that this sort of lightning did not strike often in this world.

Probably because women like her rarely existed, if ever.

Eyes closed, he indulged in her flavor, sampled the edges of her mouth, sucked her lower lip with the slightest pressure. Without thought, drawn purely by wicked impulse, his tongue ran across the lip, and once again at the seam between the two.

Her cheeks heated beneath his palms, and he worried that fear or humiliation summoned the sudden flush.

Just when he might have pulled away, she leaned closer. Stepping her feet between his, curling her fingers in his lapels.

And, like a miracle, her mouth opened beneath his, lips parting to reveal her own tentative tongue, which lapped at him with a delicate, kitten-like motion.

The sensation unstitched him completely, until a flood

of lust pounded at the seams of iron will he'd constructed within.

And still he stood against it. Against the demons that screamed to have her, pleaded to be purified in her angelic presence.

Never. He could only have this.

This moment.

This kiss.

A kiss worth waiting three decades for.

CHAPTER 7

Never had a book been written that could aptly describe the magnitude of a kiss.

Felicity's romances spent all kinds of time describing what the act might entail. How it might feel. But nothing had prepared her for the onslaught of masculine desire that was Gareth Severand. No one ever wrote about the little indescribable things.

How could they?

The flavor of heat. The glide of a tongue against another, the top textured and beneath unutterably slick and smooth. The comingling of breath that was at once damp and dry. A chill on the inhale, and a tickling warmth after.

Pressure everywhere. Gentle from his lips and exploring tongue. More insistent from other places. Secret places gone soft and disconcertingly liquid. As if a hidden dam of desire had been perforated, threatening to flood her with pleasure.

More.

She wanted more. She craved what came next, though she only had a vague sense of what that might be.

Felicity knew how physical passion culminated in the mating between a man and woman, but it was the dance in between she'd never learned the steps to.

The kisses and courtship. The *how* and *when* and *what* and *why* of it all.

Strange and outrageous urges flooded her body. She wanted to slip her hands into his jacket and test the tense ridges beneath with her fingers. Yearned to slide over and around him like a cat, rubbing every part of her flesh against his in lithe, permissive caresses.

She had the odd urge to bite him. To nibble and suck and nip and lick... to score him with her teeth and her nails. To—

An odd gleam and a dull thud stunned her, as did the abrupt broken seal of their mouths when he all but leapt away.

Blinking her eyes open, Felicity caught a glimpse of the knife embedded into the wood of the trellis beside them, still vibrating with motion.

Whereas time had seemed to stand still during their kiss, everything now raced to catch it up.

Felicity's joints were no more substantial than jelly and her brain made of little more than porridge. The air might have been quicksand for how it impeded her responses and movement.

Gareth, in contrast, reacted with twice the speed and ease of someone half his size.

A metallic flash in the lanternlight barely registered before he shoved her roughly to the ground.

Felicity landed hard, the breath knocked out of her with a startled grunt. He crouched over her in time for another blade to sail through the space their standing bodies had only just occupied. When it landed in the garden, she stared at it for a moment, imagining where it might have found purchase in her flesh.

Her chest, possibly? Or her throat.

Trying to capture control of her empty lungs, she watched her personal guard leap up like a cat, yank the first blade from the trellis, and toss it back into the direction from which it sprang.

A low grunt told her he'd hit the mark, but that didn't seem to mollify Gareth.

He whipped the tails of his coat back, pulling a dagger from some unseen sheath.

"Stay down," he ordered.

She could do nothing but.

Two men materialized from the shadows of the corner of the garden. Gareth lunged for them, leaping over the railing only to duck another thrown dagger upon landing. He crushed pansies and geraniums as he charged, and Felicity couldn't imagine the courage it must have taken for the men to stand against him.

Courage or madness.

One of them, a tall, pale fellow with thick arms for his lanky form, limped slightly, the blade in his hand dark with his own blood.

Served him right.

Though her protector wielded his own knife, he didn't use it, not immediately. Instead, he kicked out at the pale man's injured leg. It buckled beneath him and, with a strangled sound, the assailant dropped to the ground in a heap.

Gareth stood over him like the very angel of death. "Who sent you?" he demanded.

"Go to the devil, savage!"

The man's neck made the most sickening sound as Gareth stomped on it before quickly turning to his next victim. This time, their blades flashed and flickered in the dim night as they circled each other, neither of them speaking a word.

She'd never expected violence to be so quiet.

It occurred to her to go for help. To run inside and make someone contact the authorities, but her struggling lungs kept her pinned to the ground.

A third man melted from the shadows, placing his stocky form between her and Gareth. At the sight of the blade he lifted against her guard, Felicity finally found the strength to draw a frantic breath.

To warn him.

Air screamed into her lungs with agonizing labor, and the pitiable sound drew the notice of this third interloper, who turned and advanced upon her.

Panicking, Felicity remembered the knife that'd sailed past them into the garden, and struggled to her hands and knees.

She heard the clomp of a boot on the opposite end of the pergola, and looked behind her. Gareth was still across the garden, applying his blade to his opponent. The stocky blighter smiled the smile of a shark, one of a predator who knew he'd cornered his next kill. He made a sound of perverse delight as he lifted his dagger.

Felicity scrambled to the bed of moss, finding the abandoned blade.

She hadn't the slightest notion how to use it, but she had to try. Fingers wrapped around the hilt with a death grip, she thrust it in his direction.

Just in time to watch as Gareth rose behind the villain.

His fingers splayed over one side of the stocky man's face one moment before Gareth smashed his skull into the column of the pergola.

Which shattered.

The pergola *and* the skull.

Felicity turned away from the sight. Her hand clamped over her mouth as her guts rolled and bile clawed its way up her esophagus.

Blood. She hated her body's reaction to it, but knew it couldn't be helped.

"Felicity." Gareth's voice was barely a growl above a whisper. "Felicity, look at me."

She shook her head, convulsively swallowing as the

punch she'd enjoyed earlier threatened to make a ghastly reappearance.

Not now. Not in front of him.

She convulsed several times, retching all over the moss, shuddering as her body rejected everything she'd had to eat or drink over the past several hours.

A hand splayed across her back as she did so, another one supporting her, and she heaved again and again. Once she'd finished, she pulled a handkerchief from her pocket and pressed it to her mouth, just in case.

"It's over," he said in a jagged tone, this one bleak and resigned. "I need to get you out of here."

She nodded, unable to do more than that. Her lungs rebelled. Her stomach revolted. Her legs had somehow disappeared.

Rather than help her up, Gareth scooped her into his arms, and plunged into the darkness of the garden corner. They escaped out a back gate and Felicity thought she heard him mutter about undone locks allowing the brigands inside.

Once in the street, Felicity clung to his neck as he identified three horses in the alley between one great house and the next. They were not the sort of beasts any nobleman would pay a penny to own.

No question as to whom they belonged.

Before she could contest, he'd tossed her upon the back of the tallest steed, and mounted behind her.

Clinging tenaciously to the saddle, Felicity shrank back against his chest as he spurred the horse into a lurching gallop over the cobbles. They rode thunderously into the London night, their way illuminated by pallid lamps and a smattering of carriages idling in wait to convey the revelers to bed.

Felicity wasn't the horsewoman her sisters were. Despite receiving lessons from her intractable mother, she'd always had an uneasy relationship with the beasts. Prudence had once told her a horse could sense her fear, and it responded in kind.

Unable to suppress her fear, she'd decided horses were best appreciated from the ground.

Gareth, however, had no such compunctions. He rode expertly with one hand on the reins, and the other secured around her waist, cinching her to his body.

Anytime her life had been in danger, she'd obsessed over the worst outcomes, picturing herself over and over again the mangled casualty of a thousand fates.

Tonight, all she seemed to be able to focus on was the roll of his hips against her backside as they rode. The ridges and swells of his torso molded against her. It was like being buttressed by warm granite.

Her home wasn't far, and when they dashed into the courtyard, Gareth leapt from the saddle before the horse had quite stopped, reaching up to pluck her down without a modicum of assistance from her.

Once her feet were planted on the earth, he stabilized her with one hand, while turning to give the beast a hearty slap on the flanks.

The horse snorted and started before trotting back out the archway and into the London night.

"Holy Moses," she finally managed.

Propelling her toward the house, he wrenched open the door— this time unlocked— and roughly pulled her inside, slamming it behind him and throwing the latch.

"We— I— you..." She'd begun trembling in earnest now, unable to stop the deep tide of horror that threatened to tumble her beneath the waves. "We should summon someone— the police? What are you doing?"

His hands were on her, roughly turning her this way and that. "Did they hurt you? Did anything touch you?" He tested her joints and what he could see of her skin, inspecting her like some sort of rag doll.

"No," she answered immediately, then took a moment

to really examine her own body, to clench and unclench each muscle. "No. You never let them get close enough to touch me. But, Gareth... your head."

Oh no, she felt another swoon come on... or perhaps worse.

She clapped a hand over her mouth.

Blood seeped down the brutal planes of his face from a gash near his hairline. He reached up to touch it and seemed surprised to find the wound.

"I'd forgotten," he said by way of disgruntled explanation.

She whirled away from him, lurching in his grasp, grateful he didn't let her go. A second hand joined the first over her mouth as dark spots crept into her vision.

"Miss Felicity?" Mr. Bartholomew and Mrs. Pickering rushed from below stairs, the plump housekeeper reaching for Felicity. "Dear God, child, what's happened?"

She pointed back at Gareth, the tears streaming from her eyes because of her physical reaction to the blood rather than any sort of emotional distress. "He's hurt," she croaked, hoping they'd help him.

"Mr. Bartholomew, you must send for the carriage," Gareth said as if she hadn't spoken. "It's still on Barclay Street and must be retrieved quickly. It is imperative that we appear to have left with the rest of the crowd."

"Bodies!" Mrs. Pickering exclaimed.

"They... they tried to kill me." There'd been blood spilled in the dark. Her own rushed around, threatening to drown her.

"Who tried to kill you?"

"Hired thugs." Pulling a handkerchief from his coat, Gareth pressed it to the cut above his eye, bracing against her stumble. "Take her," he commanded.

Mrs. Pickering's pillowy arms surrounded Felicity, and she sagged against the woman, fighting to remain conscious. "She's right, Mr. Severand. You are bleeding rather a lot. Should I call for a doctor?"

"Care for your mistress," he clipped. "Get her out of that corset so she can breathe properly, and find a cold rag to put to her head. I'll tend to my own wound."

"Yes, sir."

Felicity wanted to call to him as he took the stairs more than two at a time, seeming to escape her without a second glance. Oh, that she could go with him, that she could clean his wounds and stitch him back together.

Why must her body be so treacherous? So weak?

"Do you think they were after you, specifically, Miss Felicity?" the housekeeper asked as she guided her through the house.

"We'll never know," she murmured. "Someone threw a knife. He... Mr. Severand. He fought them, he..."

He'd killed them all. In front of her. Two of them with his bare hands. Well... boot, in one case.

He'd done it for *her*.

"Thank God he was there," Mrs. Pickering exclaimed. "Thank God. If something happened to you, Miss Felicity, our hearts would be fair broken."

"Thank you." Now that the storm had passed. That she was safe in her home, her bones began to quake, and her teeth chattered as the imprint from his body faded.

They'd been after her. Somehow, she knew it. Once again this seemed more like a targeted attack than simple random violence.

So who had known she'd be at the ball? Who had the motive to do something so terribly violent as to send three men with sharp knives and clear intent?

"Let's get you some brandy and put you in a nightgown." Mrs. Pickering helped her up the stairs toward her bedroom.

Felicity peeked at the dark doorframe of the washroom behind which she could hear water running from the pumps.

Gareth. "Someone needs to tend to him."

"A hero, he is," Mrs. Pickering agreed. "I was dubious about him at first, but I'm glad you followed your intuition and hired the man. He'll find the brigand behind this."

Suddenly, Felicity felt sorry for the brigand.

Lord, he'd been such a gentle giant until now, she sometimes let herself forget what she'd hired him to do. He was a man who, by his own admission, claimed violence as his only skill.

He'd conducted that violence efficiently tonight without constraint or hesitation. Seemingly without thought.

Without remorse.

In fact, she recalled the look of savage triumph as he'd crushed the third villain's skull before the knife aimed at her breast could let fly.

What sort of life must he have lived to amass such expertise? To kill with such ease?

To kiss with such soul-melting tenderness.

A paradox was Gareth Severand.

One she *should* have feared after such a display.

But she didn't.

Now what she feared was being without him.

CHAPTER 8

Gareth swiped a towel over his bloodied face before throwing it into the laundry heap. He paced the expansive washroom floor for several minutes, maybe longer.

He knew the room was tiled in handsome blues and greens, with white marble floors beneath the ornate copper tub.

But he could see none of that through the mien of red.

The bloodlust refused to retract. His muscles remained engorged with violence, with the pure, carnal familiarity he had with it.

He'd killed.

He'd enjoyed it. He wanted to bring those men to life and do it again. Oh, but he'd take his time with them if he had his druthers. He'd baptize them in pain and blood before he sent them to face their eternal reckoning.

His only solace was knowing that he'd meet them in hell, and then he'd teach the devil a thing or two about punishment.

They knew better than to challenge him. At least, two of them had. Because they'd known him in a previous life.

They'd once called him their master.

Clayton Honeycutt and Richard Smythe. Both of

them skilled killers. Both of them Fauves before the organization had fallen apart upon his and Raphael's "death."

They hadn't recognized him... until it had been too late.

Christ, what did this mean? Had all of this been about him the entire time?

Was Felicity in danger, not because of her inheritance, but because of his attachment to her?

Had someone followed him as he watched over her? And if so, why decide to strike now when he'd been "dead" for a year?

Gabriel stayed in London to make certain the last of the Fauves had been dismantled. To look for Marco. And to keep her safe.

Had Marco, the wily Spaniard, somehow figured out his identity?

Did her current nightmare exist only because of him?

Had he stolen whatever peace of mind she had left only for a kiss?

That *kiss*.

What a revelation. He'd known kissing was something people did every day without thought. That lovers and spouses and sweethearts indulged in the seemingly innocuous practice on a whim.

He'd always wanted, wondered, wished...

But he'd never imagined the potent enormity of the deed. That by capturing his mouth, a woman could possess his entire body. That the intimacy of shared breath and rapturous tastes might liquify his muscle to molten iron and turn his blood into honey.

Blood.

He looked from the sink in front of him as streaks of red crawled toward the drain, to his face in the mirror above it.

His face. He still didn't recognize it. A man stared

back at him, almost entirely whole and yet not any part of him as it should be.

His nose might have been aquiline if not for the ragged bone beneath. Eyes that didn't quite match in size were shadowed by an eyebrow split by a scar.

The corner of his upper lip stitched together and healed into a slight divot, giving him an eternal appearance of cruel disdain.

It was easier, somehow, when he had looked like a fiend. When his features terrified others as effortlessly as his reputation.

When she'd fainted at the sight of him.

Easier, because he'd woken every day a monster, and surprised no one by doing monstrous things.

It seemed more honest. Man was often the worst kind of beast, and the most dangerous ones, he reckoned, were those who hid behind angelic features.

Gabriel wet the edge of another cloth and wiped at the grooves branching from his eyes, the crease of his nose and the brackets of his mouth. He dabbed at the cut below his hairline, barely worth the trouble.

The bleeding had stopped and revealed it was hardly more than a few layers of skin that'd decided to gush like a highland waterfall in spring.

Most of the blood he'd just rinsed from his hands hadn't been his own.

And she'd witnessed the slaughter.

Poor Felicity had barely been able to look at him after, had retched up a few organs in response.

He closed his eyes for a long breath as a tide of regret swamped him.

Berating himself, Gabriel wrenched open his vest and released the top buttons of his shirt, pulling it aside to assess the damage done by Honeycutt's knife.

Perhaps it was better this way, he conceded as he folded a towel and affixed it to his torso wound, applying firm pressure. Better she knew what he was capable of before anything else happened. Before he had the disastrous idea to hope for more than a kiss. To allow his thoughts and his hands to wander her body. To seek other experiences he'd thus been denied.

He'd never meant for that kiss to happen. But the moonlight and her scent, the feel of her in his arms as she led him in a graceful rhythm. Their bodies in some perfect, graceful sync. The glimmer of feminine appreciation in her eyes.

Her lips had sought *him*. She'd pressed that ghost of a caress against his mouth, and every tenuous chord he'd lashed to the final vestiges of his decency unraveled.

He'd remember the taste of her as long as he lived.

A knock on the door brought him from the mirror. The iodine, needle and thread he'd requested from the maids must have arrived.

Replacing a few buttons back over his chest, he pressed his forearm to his side to secure the makeshift bandage in place before opening the door.

Her nipples were hard.

It shouldn't have been the first thing he noticed. Not when Felicity stood there in thin layers of high-necked cream satin and lace. She held the stitching implements he'd called for in one hand and a mystery tin in the other.

Thank God she couldn't seem to bring herself to look at him, because it took a shameful moment to drag his own eyes away from the pebbled points peeking through her gown and wrapper.

Damn summer nightclothes for being so thin.

Damn his body for becoming hard as a diamond at the sight.

"What is it?" The question emerged harsher than he'd intended.

Though the scent of floral soap told him she'd washed, her hair remained dry, released from the braids of her coif and brushed into a glossy cloud of rioting fluff that fell in unruly waves past her shoulder blades.

"I was told you requested stitching, and wanted to... to check for myself that your head wound is not too serious," she told the doorframe.

Touched by her concern, he reached for her medical offerings. "It's nothing. It's not even bleeding anymore."

At that, she flicked a glance up at him from beneath her lashes before lifting her chin to properly look at him.

"Oh good." Her shoulders peeled down from her ears. "No need for these then." She brushed past him into the washroom, and discarded the needle and thread to the countertop. "I brought you a salve of honey, oregano, and goldenseal to protect it against infection."

When he reached for the tin, she pulled it from his grasp. "Please, let me."

"That's not necessary."

"It's the least I can do since you were wounded in the line of duty," she insisted. Gesturing to the wide ledge in which the tub was cast, she silently bade him to sit.

"In here?" he queried dumbly, thinking of the discarded bloody towels and the one getting bloodier beneath his shirt.

"We can go elsewhere if you wish," she suggested. "Your room, if that's more comfortab—"

"*No.*" Anyplace with a bed was a terrible idea, injured or not. "No. Here is fine."

She looked at him askance. "Very well."

He lowered himself to the ledge, suppressing a grunt, and clasped his hands in front of him to make the protection of his torso appear natural.

Felicity opened the tin and carefully bent to set the lid next to him, affording him a chance to take in the aroma of her soap and warm skin and lock it into his lungs.

Straightening to stand in front of him, she dipped two fingers into the tin and frowned. "Oh dear, the salve is a bit less congealed than I usually make." She rubbed her thumb and two fingers together, testing the texture of the stuff before lifting her hand to hover above his brow in preparation. "Here, close your eyes."

"No." The word escaped him before he thought the better of it.

She cocked her head. "But you must, you might get some of this in your eye and that would sting something horrible."

"No," he repeated, more gently this time. "I'll brave the sting if I must."

"But... but why?" She looked down at the tin. "I promise this is no ghastly potion. It's only a salve of herbs gone a bit slippery with too much tincture and not enough beeswax."

"Do you remember what you told me about fear?" he asked, tilting his chin slightly to look up at her. "I cannot bring myself to close my eyes. I have this need. This... proclivity. No matter what, I *must* see what is coming at me. I must not be caught unaware."

"I understand." He could feel her sympathetic gaze touching at the many parts of his ruined face, and he wished the caress was real. "You live a life where weapons fly at you from the dark. It's no small wonder to me you don't want to miss a thing."

After such an admission of his weakness, he couldn't seem to summon a reply.

She bent closer, her whisper both consoling and conspiratorial. "It is only you and me here. Nothing unseen. Nothing in the shadows."

That didn't matter, his soul still itched to crawl out of his skin at the thought of giving up a sense that he relied upon to fight.

"Trust me, Mr. Severand."

Trust. It was a word he didn't recognize. A concept he never learned.

"I would never hurt you. I promise."

She didn't understand that she was the only person alive who truly could.

Watching her retch in the garden, his heart had bled along with the rest of him. She hadn't been able to look at him without being sick. What he'd done, who he was, repulsed and dismayed her. As it should.

He'd murdered three men.

"Please?" she pled, her expression beseeching. "You saved my life tonight, and I… I must do something for you. I cannot sleep if I think your wound might fester."

Denying her, it seemed, was something he was incapable of doing.

Taking in a deep breath, he let his lids fall.

He couldn't suppress a flinch when she touched his shoulder, but as her hand rested there to steady herself, he found that connection of their bodies made him almost preternaturally aware of what she did. His other senses roared to life, experiencing her in ways he'd not yet done.

Her scent imbued him with lavender and something sharper emanating from the tin. The scratch of satin against his trousers as she moved between his legs was possibly the most erotic sensation of his life. The soft feathering of breath against his hair. The chilly glide of the salve over the scratch, her touch barely more detectable than a butterfly's wing. The throaty murmur of compassionate encouragement. Bereft of words but full of meaning.

Gabriel swallowed a groan.

"This is not so deep as I thought it might be," she remarked, using a soft cloth to catch a drop of the salve before it ran into his eyebrow.

"Head wounds tend to bleed more than others, appearing worse than they are initially."

"Oh." She applied a second coat of the stuff, being exceedingly thorough.

Or, perhaps, lingering? It'd no doubt been a traumatizing night for her, perhaps she was frightened to be alone. Perhaps she'd come to him seeking solace, something he'd never quite had to give.

"What you saw tonight... what happened... I wish I could express how sorry I am that you had to witness—"

"Can I tell you something?" she interrupted, her voice as steady as he'd ever heard it.

"Of course." He wanted to know everything about her.

"Tonight was terrifying. But I wasn't sick because of what you did. I mean, I was, but it's the blood, you see. The sight of blood makes me ill, sometimes enough that I faint."

At that, his eyes opened. Could it be all this time, her reactions had not to do with him? Even when she'd looked upon his face after the Midnight Masquerade...

He'd been splattered with the blood he shed to get her out.

"But you volunteer at a hospital," he wondered aloud.

Her gaze skittered away. "I thought if I was around blood and such all the time, I'd inure myself to it. But after so many swoons, I was considered more of a risk than a help, and was delegated to sit with people as they recovered, and assist with paperwork." She brightened as she reached for the lid of the tin. "I also create herbal tinctures that my brother-in-law Dr. Conleith uses as remedies for his patients' more treatable ills."

"Oh? And what do you make?" She must be particularly good, as upon application of the salve, the smarting of his head wound ceased.

"Well, mustard and comfrey poultices for chest ailments. Peppermint and wintergreen tinctures for sinus and lungs. Valerian and chamomile for soothing nerves. Fennel, mint, and licorice root for stomach remedies.

Raspberry leaves and evening primrose oil for... well, for feminine ailments. And this, an antiseptic for wounds. Titus said it's been a godsend."

"That is why you spend so much time in the greenhouse," he realized, remembering a few afternoons and evenings he'd been brave enough to linger in the courtyard archway to see her tend her numerous plants.

"That, among other things."

"What other things?"

She wiped her fingers on the cloth, and he noted that she'd not yet moved from between his knees. "Just whatever strikes my fancy, I suppose. I like the speed at which things grow."

"Speed?" He lifted an inquiring brow.

Her lashes swept down. "I suppose that's the wrong word for it. Less speed... more fortitude. Plants are so fickle sometimes, so delicate, and often need very specific care. But at the same time, they can be so determined to bloom. To find a way. I like to think I can help. There's something lovely about plunging my fingers in the soil. I appreciate the smell and the textures. I love tiny veins on the leaves and the imperceptible movements of the buds. Some follow the sun, but you never see them move. It's a world so fascinating to me, one full of life and yet so still and silent. It is where I feel useful, but not necessary."

Retrieving a small sticking plaster from the sink, she returned to apply it, catching her tongue in the corner of her lip as she concentrated. "My secret for this salve is tea tree. It will help with scarring."

"What is one more scar?" he asked wryly.

She puffed out a breath of mirth and it washed him in goosebumps. Her lips were right there. Every muscle in his body knew it.

"Mr. Severand!" She grabbed at his sleeve, and he looked down to see a dark red blotch on it. "You're cut!"

"It's nothing, I'll look after it when you're done here."

"Why didn't you say so? Oh, dear God."

The cloth he'd been holding over the slash had tumbled to the ground at their feet when she'd seized upon his arm. He'd bled through the thin material, as she'd stayed longer than he'd expected her to.

"I'm— I'm sorry." Her legs gave out suddenly and he caught her before she tumbled to the floor. Suddenly limbless, she slid down his body.

Her blueberry eyes went almost comically wide beneath her spectacles as they each became abruptly aware of the erection pulsing between them.

Gabriel forgot to breathe. She had no panels. No corset. Nothing but billowing fabric between her breasts and his cock.

Christ. It felt amazing.

Felicity, on the other hand, visibly lost control of her lungs, expanding and contracting her ribs against the insistently hard flesh between them. Her pupils dilated so large, the black threatened to swallow all that cerulean with a darkness that didn't belong on her features.

Was she astonished? Shocked? Displeased? Offended?

Aroused?

Certainly not.

He reached for her shoulders, intent upon helping her to stand. Hoping she wouldn't be sick.

Instead, she fainted.

Gabriel caught her and leaned her against his good side as he used his shirt to tie a bandage on the slash.

Grunting in pain as he picked her up, he carried her to her chamber and settled her on the bed, pulling up the covers and tucking them beneath her chin.

In every fantasy he ever had, he crawled in beside her.

"Goodnight, Felicity."

Taking a liberty he didn't deserve, he bent to plant a kiss on her forehead before escaping back to the washroom.

Ripping off his ruined, knotted shirt, he went about the tedious and painful job of washing his wound and stitching it up using the mirror and one-handed magic. It wasn't the pierce of the needle that set his teeth on edge, but the sensation of the thread running through the skin.

He gritted through it, only requiring six stitches in all. Once he'd finished, he swiped some of the salve on the wound before layering gauze over it and wrapping a bandage around his rib cage to keep it in place.

This would be good as new in two weeks or less.

The entire time, he'd expected his arousal to abate. The pain should have deflated it, the tedium of the stitching and, yes, the sight of his own blood.

But nothing would, it seemed. He'd been in some state of arousal since they'd kissed. Even while killing her enemies. Even while hating and berating himself.

All his cock seemed to do was consistently pulse with increasingly incessant demand.

He looked at his torso in the mirror, etched with tattoos and bound with gauze, at the tiny plaster below his hairline.

God, he was such a fool. To have imagined a sexual response in her eyes? In what sort of dream did he exist?

He'd never had a woman so close to him before. Never felt the soft curves of a female body pressed against his. Never thought of the erotic cleft between breasts as a place for his cock to find pleasure.

A surge of agonizing lust weakened his knees.

Unable to stop himself, he released the placket of his trousers and licked his palm before gripping himself. Biting his lip against the pleasure/pain of flesh too long denied, he worked his hand over his cock.

Arching his neck, he leaned his hip against the counter, and closed his eyes.

The rough skin of his hand was a hollow solace, incomparable to her softness. The grip of his palm, the only pleasure familiar to him, was often quick and efficient.

Something to alleviate pressure.

This time, he caressed his own skin as he imagined she might do. Running from base to tip with long, slow strokes. He knew the images pouring down behind the backs of his eyelids were degrading to her innocent loveliness.

But now he knew the warmth of her touch, the curiosity of her tongue, the slick magic found in the depths of her delectable mouth. How would those perfect, Cupid's-bow lips look stretched to wrap around the head of his...

The sharp jolt of a climax sliced through him, this one gathering from nowhere and striking like a blade in the dark.

His limbs locked, his hand quickening its pace as now, in his mind's eye, those breasts were exposed. Pink-tipped and lovely.

He gasped and wrenched as pleasure pulled liquid warmth from his body, imagining anointing her flesh with it.

Of her accepting the slick leavings of his lust in her mouth, on her breasts.

Fuck. He was an animal for wishing such things upon her.

And yet, he'd return the favor. He would do anything for her. To her. He'd debase himself to a ridiculous degree if she asked him.

Or better yet, commanded him.

Christ. Nothing would please him more.

And nothing could be further from a possibility than making love to Felicity Goode.

CHAPTER 9

A WEEK LATER

Felicity used the sound of the water pump to cover that of her tears.

She'd kept them at bay until Titus left after unwittingly dropping a fragmenting explosive into the middle of her already shattered nerves.

By habit, she searched for Gareth in the garden beyond the endless beads of rain sluicing down the glass enclosure on all sides. He'd made himself scarce the moment her brother-in-law had appeared in the courtyard to deliver his news in the glasshouse.

No doubt, her personal guard meant to give her some privacy with her family, but it appeared that he'd quite vanished.

Because he never shirked his duty, she knew he was nearby.

And yet at a distance.

Almost a week had gone since the ball, and she'd never felt more alone in her life. The morning after their kiss— after she'd fainted quite literally *on him*— she'd awoken to check and see if his wound was all right.

If they were all right.

And it seemed while Gareth's rib was sutured and healing nicely, that evening had driven something between them. Though he was civil and responsive to her needs and suggestions, Gareth had become like a fortress against a siege, cold and impenetrable.

Infuriatingly polite.

He'd gone back to calling her *Miss Goode*, which felt like a slap in the face every time. At the four subsequent events they'd attended, he'd found a way to avoid touching her. Even stepping by to allow the footmen to hand her down from carriages or take her cloak.

Their every interaction had been monosyllabic at best.

She hated it.

Filling her brass watering can, Felicity hauled it with shaking limbs to her rosemary. It wasn't lost on her, the irony that she watered plants by hand when the deluge outside might have done just as well.

It didn't matter. So many things wilted in the chill and wind. They were not meant to withstand the unrelenting weather. All they needed was a bit of shelter from the cold to thrive.

A tending hand and an observant gardener to coax their shy blooms from hiding.

Who would look after them if anything were to happen to her?

The only other person who knew a whit about their care was Mrs. Winterton… and she… she…

Oh, God.

The can slipped from her grip and fell to the stone footpath with a rancorous crash, spilling water in every direction.

Overcome and overwrought, Felicity buried her face in her hands and sobbed.

Gareth was there within seconds, his hands on her shoulders, her wrists, pulling them from her face to search for a wound. "Are you hurt?"

There he was. For just a moment, those icy grey eyes had melted with concern. His gaze touched every single part of her face, her hands front and back, the corpse of the overturned watering can. "What the bloody hell happened?"

All she wanted to do was to step into the circle of his arms, to press her cheek against the strength of his chest and release the storm of tears that'd been gathering for so long. Because she knew what it felt like now, the warmth and muscle that resided there.

How would it be to find shelter beneath such a buttress of fortitude? To cast her burdens on his Sisyphean shoulders, for surely they were capable of bearing her weight if only to give her a moment to breathe.

She wouldn't do it. Not when he so distinctly drew a line in the sand between them.

It was for the best, surely.

"What did Conleith say to make you cry?" he demanded, scowling toward the arch with a very dark sort of wrath.

"E-Emmaline... Mrs. W-Winterton. She's taken a turn for the worse. She's in so much pain, Titus had to sedate her. He's worried that if she can't keep down any water, her organs might fail."

His expression changed from one of frantic fury to troubled bemusement. "You said she was well when you visited her yesterday."

Nodding, she gathered up her apron to wipe at the eyes that wouldn't stop leaking. "She was! Though a bit pale and worn, she sat up as we had an entire conversation."

Gently, without interrupting her, Gareth pulled her gardening apron from her fingers and pressed a clean handkerchief to them.

Grateful, she wiped at her nose, and did her best to beat back the storm of fear and emotion threatening to engulf her. "Emmaline was feeling strong and said she would be ready to come home soon. She stood to embrace me before I left the hospital and whispered into my ear that I was her closest friend. She promised to always love and protect me. And now..." Anguish welled up in her eyes and overflowed in a new onslaught of grief. "What if that was the last time I ever see my friend? All because *I* failed to protect *her*."

Collapsing against him, she did what she'd promised herself she wouldn't, and wet his shirtfront with her tears.

His hands rested on her spine. Not an embrace, but a semblance of comfort. Strong, surprisingly lithe fingers smoothed up and down her back in a gentle caress that was as hesitant as it was reassuring.

"What could you have possibly done to protect Mrs. Winterton?" His voice sounded impossibly deeper when pressed against the chest that produced it. It vibrated through her with a consoling rumble.

"Titus is convinced her ailment isn't stemming from poorly prepared food. He... he suspects she was poisoned."

He made a pensive sound. "Does Mrs. Winterton have enemies? Could she have ingested something on her mysterious family journey that day?"

She shook her head, burrowing deeper against him. His shirt was damp with rain and smelled of loamy earth and spices and... whatever delicious musk radiated from his skin.

Why was she noticing things like that at a time like this?

"Not likely. I distinctly remember her saying she was famished. That she didn't have a bit to eat that day until—"

Recognition lanced her at the selfsame moment every part of him went rigid. They each pulled away long enough to look at each other and reveal their thoughts. "The fish stew."

She put a hand to her head. "I gave her my portion, and you didn't partake more than a bite because you are not fond of fish." Felicity noted the rain had bunched his forelocks into gathers of hair that still dripped water below his eyes to run down the crags and planes of his brutally compelling features. "Did you feel at all ill?"

He shook his head. "My life's left me with an iron stomach and most toxins take a larger dose to fell a man my size than a slight lady such as Mrs. Winterton or..."

His gaze skittered away.

"Or me," she breathed. "They were trying to poison me. That's what you think, isn't it?"

He didn't answer, but his hands stilled on her back before bunching into the fabric.

"I need to get my estate in order," she realized. "What if something truly happens to me? There are those in my household to worry about."

"Yes," he clipped, "Someone in your employ is likely trying to kill you."

She went very still as his words sank in and struck a chord so painful, she couldn't even fathom it.

Jerking out of his grip, she whirled away. "That's impossible."

"It's the only possibility at this point. That letter was left in your private solarium. The poison in your food. Even the fact that you were accosted at a specific time of night." His massive hand clamped on her shoulder and turned her around. "Your assailant knew where you were going to be, because someone in your household provided them that information."

Both her hands covered her mouth in sheer horror. Every part of her rejected the very notion. However, his logic was sound. "What should I do?"

"You should let every last one go."

That brought her brows down and she released her mouth to frown at him. "I can't just... I mean... some of these people have been in the house longer than I've been alive. It's their home. I refuse to punish them all for the transgression of one. Not without surety of their guilt. Don't ask that of me."

He scowled in kind, but ultimately relented. "What about a sabbatical? You could fabricate a reason to at least get them all out of the house for a time, whilst we conduct an investigation. Maybe pick one or two of your most trusted to remain. Mrs. Pickering, perhaps."

She nodded, feeling dazed. "Yes. And Mr. Bartholomew. Unless they were part of— oh, Lord. That isn't worth thinking about. What is happening?"

A band of steel surrounded her lungs and threatened to squeeze the life out of her. Heart racing and vision blurring, she worried the starch would abandon her knees.

"Felicity." His hands bracketed her shoulders, his grip careful but firm. "Felicity, listen to me."

She looked up at him, compelled by the gravitas in his voice. "Do not panic. I will keep you safe. I will watch who is left. Do you believe that?"

She did. Without question. "It's just... I wish I didn't need you to." She gripped his forearms and captured his gaze, needing to unburden herself. To explain. To apologize. To ward off the self-recrimination that'd become a part of her everyday conversation since back before she could remember.

"How is this happening to me? I've always done the right thing. I've always done the *safe* thing. I've been afraid of letting myself misbehave because then my life would truly have no meaning. I would have no use to anyone. My parents, my peers, my sisters. I convinced myself I'm capable of taking on this immense responsibility left to me by my father, but I'm discovering that the more threatened I feel, the less capable I am, and I... I detest that about myself. I really do. I can't even help *you* stitch a wound without fainting. I can't face people for longer than a few hours before I want to collapse. I'm weak and ineffectual and—"

"Stop."

She blinked up at him, stunned by his none-too-gentle tone and the firm shake he gave her.

"Listen to me, Felicity Goode," he said in a voice she'd not yet heard from him. One that could have commanded legions. "You are capable of things I've never before seen in this world. You've taught me something as I've watched you. That strength— real strength— is quiet. And that nothing is so powerful as gentility. To remain soft in a hard world, that takes immense courage. Courage few people possess. Trust me on this, Felicity, and please do not tear yourself apart over what you should not change. Do not let anyone make you feel weak for *caring*."

His words brought a very different sort of tears to her eyes, and she stared up at him with a longing she couldn't at all identify. When he was near, when he touched her… she didn't feel so hollow. She could believe that she possessed courage.

He made her brave.

"Can we forget what happened the night of the ball?" she blurted, silently pleading with him to melt the fortress of ice between them. "I don't want there to be this uncomfortable distance. I miss the ease of what we had before."

Severity and relief sat strangely on features such as his. "I do as well," he admitted.

"Then let us chalk it up to a strange and dangerous evening. One we needn't think on further."

"That seems best."

"Thank you." She threw her arms around his middle, careful not to press against his wound.

He did not return her embrace, but she understood

her uncharacteristic surge of affection was neither appropriate nor expected. Pulling away, she bent to retrieve her watering can. "After I finish this, will you stand with me while I break the news to the staff?"

"Whatever you need." He glanced around at the flowers and ferns, whose leaves and blossoms reached from their pots as if in hopes of touching him like adoring devotees. "May I help with your plants?"

"No one has ever offered to assist me before." She handed him the watering pot and retrieved a much smaller misting tool.

He lifted a shoulder and pivoted, almost upsetting a ficus. "If you are in need of assistance, you can always call upon me. Even if it's something you worry I might find menial."

Touched, she turned away so he wouldn't see the glow in her heart shining out through her eyes.

She'd lied to him, of course. There was no forgetting what they'd done at the ball.

Just like the sight of a giant like him tending to her beloved flora...

That kiss would stay with her forever.

CHAPTER 10

It surprised Felicity just how quickly her house emptied beneath Gareth's watchful eye. By the time the sun went down, only Pickering and Bartholomew were left, and Gareth had gone below stairs to the kitchens to supervise a delivery of food and preparation for their evening meal.

The four of them ate together in a small nook off the kitchens with a lovely view of the courtyard and garden.

Felicity quite enjoyed the pelt of rain on the windows and a simple dish of roasted squab and charred asparagus. She'd always been quite fond of Mrs. Pickering, and the woman made her feel better as they spoke of Emmaline and darker things.

The housekeeper even toiled to pull Gareth into the conversation, asking about his childhood and such.

Though he was polite, he didn't seem inclined to divulge.

Felicity had the sense his was not a childhood worth remembering.

The chime at the door interrupted their evening card game, which Felicity had a sneaking suspicion Gareth was letting them win.

He stalked Mr. Bartholomew to the door like a menacing shadow, his body tensed and ready for just about anything the night could bring to their landing.

Anything, but two screaming twins and a harried nursery maid.

"Effie? What's happened?" Felicity rushed down the corridor toward their entry, where the maid wouldn't even relinquish her coat.

"Me mam's gone missing," she sniffed, rainwater dripping from her cap. "She gets lost sometimes, see. Sir and Lady Morley left these little bitties in my care while they gone off to some to do wots thrown by the police and politicians and it is most of the household's 'alf day. I can't take 'em to the doc and Lady Nora on account of her bedrest and he's cutting out some other woman's little 'un. I thought maybe since you had a household full of staff—"

"Of course, you were right to bring them here." Felicity plucked little Charlotte from the double-slotted pram and thrust her into Gareth's arms before she turned back to gather up little Caroline. "Go see to your mother, Effie; we'll be fine until their parents return."

Effie, a bosomy, wiry-haired woman who might have been thirty-five or fifty, eyed Gareth with a suspicious sniff. "You sure everything is all right here?" she asked.

Felicity had been torn about what she should divulge to her sister and Morley since they'd returned only two days prior from the Continent. She was supposed to see them for a family dinner on Saturday, and decided to introduce the family to Gareth— and her predicament—all at once.

It wouldn't do to have Effie take information of a frightening-looking gentleman back to the Morleys.

Thankfully, Mrs. Pickering rushed forward and handed Effie some warm bread and provisions to take into the cold.

Gareth, still gripping the wriggling, squalling child beneath both armpits, offered her to the housekeeper, who simply chucked the infant under her chins. "Their teeth are still coming in, poor mites. We've two boiled bottles and a wee bit of goat's milk for them to suckle."

The thunderstruck look of desperation on Gareth's face as the woman disappeared down the hall would be locked in Felicity's vault of amusing memories henceforth and forever.

"Look here." She tucked the baby against her chest, pulling the blanket into a makeshift swaddle and patting her little bum as she cradled and bounced her. "Just like this, watch her head, and don't jostle her over much. She'll calm down in a bit."

With slow, painful movements, he mimicked her hold, but it didn't seem to have the effect it should, as little Charlotte only became more upset.

He made a face. "I don't think I—"

"No, you're doing fine, just put your arm beneath her. Yes, like that. Let's go through to the parlor."

She turned away from him, needing a moment to compose herself after the sight of him with a drooling, chubby infant caused an explosion of butterfly wings in the vicinity of her womb.

She went to the settee and sat, rocking the quieting child in her arms as she cooed to it. "There you are, little one." She caressed the girl's tiny brow, ran her fingertip along the bridge of her nose. "You're out of the cold now. You're with Aunt Felicity, what fun we shall have."

Instead of taking up his regular seat across the way, Gareth sank down beside her. Watching her carefully and imitating her every move.

"What's it doing now?" The note of uncharacteristic distress in his voice had her fighting a smile.

"Just untangle the blanket so she can move," Felicity gently corrected. "And it is a *her,* and *her* name is Charlotte."

He laid the baby longways on his lap, supporting her head between his knees as he unwrapped her busy limbs. As small fists windmilled and little feet kicked out in grateful freedom, he glanced from baby to baby with stern consternation. "How can you tell them apart?"

"You might not know this, but *I* am a twin. That makes me extra qualified, I imagine."

"You don't say."

She couldn't be certain, but it seemed he very studiously avoided her gaze.

"I mentioned my sister Mercy. The one who is traveling." The twinge of sadness took her by surprise. She missed Mercy every day, but this evening, their separation was like a physical ache.

What would Mercy think of Gareth Severand?

"You do not like that she's with her husband?" he asked alertly.

She shook her head as Caroline's little fist closed over her finger. "I don't like that he took her from my side. But I told her to go. She's so happy. She's having all the adventures she yearned for since we were young. And I'm glad of it."

"And her marriage? Her husband? Are you glad of that?"

She glanced over to see him holding his hands out as little pads for Charlotte's strong kicks. The baby seemed delighted with this, and was instantly cheerful.

"I can't say I know him well," Felicity admitted, attracted in every way by the sight of him with a child in his lap. Soothed by his presence. By the fact that they sat so close. "I'll be honest, I have my concerns. He was a—well, an infamously unscrupulous man most of his life. But I believed him when he said he loved her. I don't think I've ever believed anything so much as that."

In fact, she always wished a man would look at her like Raphael Sauvageau looked at Mercy.

Like she was his greatest treasure.

"And... does your sister return his love?" He seemed more interested in the answer than she suspected he would be. How nice, to have a man pay such good attention to a conversation not about himself.

"Oh yes, she's nigh gone for him."

"How do you know if you are not together?"

Felicity snorted. "Her letters are mostly swooning, elated stanzas of praise for him. And I'm glad of it."

"You do not seem so glad."

She looked down at the bundle in her arms, convinced that Caroline, such a peaceful child, might take after herself. Would she only be an aunt for the rest of her days? Might no one ever call her Mother? "If I'm honest, I'm envious. Mercy always claimed she'd never marry. She made me promise not to, either. We were going to make our own way in this world the same way we came into it. Together. And here we are... here I am... beholden to duty while her choice has somehow granted her a modicum of freedom."

She cleared a gather of bitterness from her throat at the same time Charlotte made an adoring noise up at Gareth.

"I think she likes you," she murmured when the child curled a strong, chubby fist around one of his rough fingers.

"How can you tell?"

"Look at her face, she's very contented."

"Well..." His nose wrinkled in a wry grimace. "That might have been the bubbles I just felt coming out of the back end."

Felicity threw her head back and laughed in a burst of pure merriment. How easily he could dispel her earlier melancholy with his dry wit. And her loneliness with his very presence.

When she finally looked over at Gareth, he'd gone perfectly still.

And was smiling at her. An honest-to-goodness smile. Both sides of his lips relaxed into something that looked like joy.

It was like standing in the sun for the first time. Warm and beautiful and breathtaking.

"Haven't you ever held a child before?" she asked, glancing away and clenching her thighs.

"Never."

"At your age? I find that hard to believe."

His smile melted into mock effrontery. "I'm no Methuselah."

"How old are you?"

"All of four-and-thirty," he sniffed, obviously offended.

"It's not your age that surprises me, just that you've never been around children. There are only twelve years between us and that's no significant difference, I think."

"I should think not."

Charlotte chose that moment to shove his captured finger into her mouth and chew on it with ruthless vigor, drawing his attention.

"I'm too big a meal for you, little one," he chuffed. "But gnaw away if it makes you feel better."

Charlotte cooed, smiling and drooling on his hand.

"Would you look at that, your sister's raising a little cannibal." He checked to see if Felicity witnessed the spectacle, a winsome smirk of pride smoothing out the savage planes of his face. Producing handsome branches at the corners of his eyes and deepening the lines of his mouth.

Oh, she was looking.

She was looking in a way she'd never looked at him before. Her skin tingled and tightened around her bones and suddenly she was aware of all things that made her a woman. Her breasts became heavy, aching, the tips tightening to an almost painful degree. All the moisture deserted her mouth but pooled between her thighs. Thighs that yearned to open and clench simultaneously.

This man. He claimed to have no children. No family. And it seemed like a travesty that the world would keep existing without his child in it.

What a waste of all that masculine perfection.

Dear lord, how alarming that her body seemed to be petitioning for the job without her permission.

Felicity might be innocent, but she now understood why authors described lust as hunger. It was so physical and base. So consuming. When one needed to eat, the body and brain rarely allowed any function until the hunger was sated. The need was obsessive. Overwhelming.

So, too, was this.

Her entire being thrummed with awareness. With desire. And it would be impossible to think of anything else until she either got the hunger under control…

Or filled that emptiness with Gareth Severand.

CHAPTER 11

Gareth couldn't measure the depth of his relief when the housekeeper returned holding warm glass bottles with little rubber nipples.

She fussed and bossed him as he fed… *Oh, shit.* He'd forgotten which one he'd been holding. Caroline? Catherine? Charlotte?

It wouldn't do to ask either of the ladies, who handled the little ones with expert care. Not when they seemed so delighted with him.

Looking down at the small human in his lap, he was struck by an odd sense of wonder. The child stared back at him with eyes the startling color of Felicity's, her fingers inelegantly gripped the bottle, even as he held it steady. Her lips sealed around the nipple as she gnawed on it rather than suckled. He ran a single finger over thin black curls through which he could see her round head.

It was difficult to believe, to *comprehend* the size of her toes, even though they were right in front of him. How did one's feet go from looking like a mangled dumpling to the useful appendages people so relied upon? How did something so plump, dimpled, and creased with rolls, stretch into a whole person?

How was it possible that he'd once been like this? Small. Helpless.

It was due to his mother and a few miracles that he and Raphael survived.

He almost hadn't. So many times. His father would not have minded his demise so long as he profited from it.

The mirror had told that story until recently.

"'Tis nice to have a man about the house again." Mrs. Pickering's comment drew his notice to where she stood over him, beaming down with an approving smile. "Despite the circumstances."

He nodded his thanks, not exactly knowing what to do with a compliment. "Do we have a place for them to sleep?" he asked.

"Well certainly, but you have to burp her first."

Certain he misunderstood, he cocked his head. "I have to... what?"

"Prop her on your shoulder and give her a few swats."

His jaw dropped. He'd heard of the aristocracy having some odd and alarming child-rearing practices, but this? "I am *not* striking an infant."

At that she crowed a laugh. "Like this, you dolt." Plucking the girl from Felicity's arms, she propped the baby up on her shoulder and gave her a few firm pats on the back. "Where did ye find this oaf?"

Felicity's breathy laugh joined in. "I found him in the archway, and I'm ever so glad I did."

The warm spark the evening had ignited in his chest expanded to a glow that rivaled that of a good whisky.

"Now you try, lad," Pickering instructed. "Like so."

Hesitantly, he propped up the little mop-haired angel and cupped his hands, gently patting her on the shoulders and back.

Both women sighed in tandem, which drew his brows together in puzzlement.

"Am I doing it wrong?"

A rude little sound erupted next to his ear, followed by a warm spread of something on his collar and down his back.

His eyes went wide as a sour smell followed. "Oh fuck. I mean— shite. I mean... sorry, ladies. Is it— she— all right? Did I—"

"Don't fret, my boy, it's something babies like to do from time to time." The housekeeper bounced Caroline, her apple cheeks bunched in an endlessly amused smile.

Felicity surged to her feet and bent over him, lifting the baby from his shoulder. The darling miscreant looked oddly pleased with herself as she plucked at a lock of his hair before she was dragged away from him.

Tucking the child against her hip, Felicity wiped at the corners of the baby's mouth and was unable to cover a giggle at his dumbstruck expression. "I'm so sorry she soiled you. Please don't be cross."

"I'm not." He shrugged. "I've been soiled with worse."

He couldn't identify what he saw in her expression before she hid it from him. Something like distress, or maybe desire... Perhaps he needed his own vision checked. "You'll be wanting to clean up." She pointed to the door. "Mrs. Pickering and I will set things to rights here."

Gareth could do nothing but nod as he took in the tableau before him. Golden lamps created a halo around Felicity's corona of hair. The calming silver, ivory, and grey of the room contrasted with the violet of her dress, which somehow painted her eyes the same shade.

The child in her arms splayed a hand over her peach-tinted cheek, hooking a finger into her mouth, which caused her to laugh and nibble at the tiny fingers. "Look what you've done to poor Mr. Severand, Charlotte," she cooed. "You certainly take after your aunt Mercy."

Burbling nonsense, the baby rested her forehead

against Felicity's, who closed her eyes, apparently reveling in the sweet affection of the gesture.

Someone would make her a mother someday.

Some fucking lucky bastard would plant a baby inside of her. Would watch her form that child with her miraculous body. Would hold their progeny with pride.

The very thought made him ill.

"Pardon me then, ladies." Before he could return Charlotte's dubious favor and be sick all over, he spun on his heel and quit the room.

Gabriel took his time bathing and dressing, castigating himself for his ludicrous sentiments.

The urge to kill any man who touched her, integrating with all the reasons he refused to do so became a tumultuous vortex of frustration directed only at himself.

He wanted nothing so much as her happiness.

He wanted nothing so much as *her*... which would very probably destroy her chances at happiness.

Life had defeated him, even before he'd been born.

By the time he'd bathed, dressed, groomed, and ventured back to the main floor, Cresthaven Place was silent and almost dark as Mrs. Pickering bustled about dousing the lamps.

She greeted him with a smile and a wink. "Sir and Lady Morley came to collect their little 'uns not a half hour ago."

"I see." He looked at the closed parlor door, wondering if Felicity read behind it.

"She's gone up to bed," the observant woman informed him. "But there's some smoked meats, cheeses, and fresh bread in the kitchens. Me husband, Gordon, was a man your size. Before he died of the cholera, he was always wanting an extra meal before turning in. Near ate me into the poorhouse, God rest his soul." She adjusted her cap and winked up at him. "You remind me a bit of him, if you'd believe it. Rough hands. Hard jaw. Soft heart."

Gareth wanted to correct her, but couldn't bring himself to naysay a kind widow.

His heart had been hard for as long as he could remember. Hard and cold and withered.

"Thank you." He lingered at the banister at the bottom of the stairs, studying Mrs. Pickering for a moment. If she had anything to do with the nefarious goings on in this house, he'd never trust his instincts again. "If you had to guess how poison could have made it to the kitchens, who would you say was the likely culprit?"

The woman's dark eyes misted with remorse. "Can't imagine a one of us doing such a thing. Especially to poor Miss Felicity. Ask any of us and you'll get the same answer; whoever hurts that angel of a girl deserves to go to the devil."

"In that we agree." He turned to climb the stairs.

"Mr. Severand?" Mrs. Pickering called after him.

"Yes?"

"Thank you... for keeping her safe. I wish she could find a man like you rather than those dandies her father would have her stuck with. The two of you would be a right blessing of a master and mistress."

Gabriel snorted. "You and I both know I'm not worthy enough to lick her boots, Mrs. Pickering."

"That's part of why you're ideal." She made a caustic gesture. "Most men think they're God's gift to women, when it's actually the other way around. Someone should be so lucky to catch her heart, and that heart was in her eyes when she looked at you tonight."

He wished she wouldn't have said that. "You know that if she took up with a man like me, she'd lose everything. You, this house, her security." Her innocence, what fragile peace of mind she possessed, her reputation and good name. Possibly even her soul. "Good night, Mrs. Pickering."

"Goodnight, lad." She sighed, before her words followed him up the stairs. "These Goode girls have all learned that some things are worth giving up…"

He didn't reply, merely climbed the endless stairs to the third floor with heavy steps.

Not for the likes of me.

CHAPTER 12

The creak of a floorboard tore Gabriel from a troubled sleep.

Bolting upright, he listened to the dark. Seconds ticked by in silence, and just as he'd begun to wonder if the sound had been in his dreams, he alerted to movement on the stairs.

Leaping up, he pulled on his trousers, punched his fists into a shirt, and seized his pistol.

When Gabriel killed, he'd rather the death be silent. And wet. But he would take no chances with her life, when swift and lethal violence might be more efficient.

Pressing his ear to the door, he heard nothing on the other side, so he burst out and drew down one length of the hall, then the other.

All was silent and still.

He went to her room. Hesitated, and then remembered that hesitation got people killed.

Bursting in, he found her bedsheets rumpled.

And empty.

"Felicity?" He searched every dark corner of her room. In the wardrobe. Checked the windows, finding them locked.

The sound of a door echoed from downstairs.

He leapt into the hall and flew down the staircase in time to see the edges of light disappear from the back of the house. Spinning toward the hallway, he spied a tiny glow in the courtyard through the glass panes in the back entry. He reached the courtyard in seconds.

The glow had dimmed, now that it was contained within the glasshouse.

A lone lantern cast vague shadows of leaves and blooms on the cobbles, interrupted by the motions of a girl in a white nightgown.

Lowering his weapon, Gabriel looked up to see flashes of Felicity as she fluttered around the greenhouse like a trapped butterfly.

When he wrenched open the door, she whirled, eyes wide with a terror he'd never before seen, brandishing a trowel at him as if it were a rapier.

Relieved to find her alone, he stepped inside, the flagstones cool beneath his bare feet.

He pinpointed the moment she recognized him through eyes made opaque by whatever awful force held her in thrall. Breathing as if she'd run a league at full tilt, she dropped the sharp garden instrument and bent over, resting her palms on her knees.

Gabriel went to her, discarding his pistol on the orderly workbench behind her. "What's wrong. What happened?"

"I can't breathe. I can't... I'm..." She shuddered and sank to her knees, trembling and sweating and gulping for air.

Catching her by the shoulders, he followed her down, supporting her weight. "Did you take something? Eat something? Are you ill?"

"No," she gasped. "No. I'm sorry. I'm sorry I— I'm broken. Please leave me. It will pass."

It will pass. She'd said that in the gardens.

His heart rate slowed several degrees as he realized she didn't fight a seizure, an injury, or a toxin.

Only her own demons.

She'd told him she had episodes of terror, but he'd never imagined they could be so powerful as this.

She surged against him, burrowing into his chest like a kitten seeking warmth, and he could do nothing but curl his body around her, creating a shelter.

"You are safe. I have you." He cupped her head to his chest with one hand, the other spanning her trembling spine. "Slow your breath."

"I can't," she gasped. "My skin is on fire and my limbs are so cold. My throat will close, I feel it. *Oh, God.*"

"I won't let that happen," he soothed, watching the pulse jump in her neck like a caged hummingbird. "Just breathe with me." He deliberately expanded his ribs, then contracted them, urging her to do the same.

At first, her inhales were wobbly. Hitching and much too fast, but she did as he bade her to do. She focused. And after several silent minutes, her breaths matched the rhythm of his with only a few hiccups.

The tremors in her limbs gentled and she melted against him in a boneless drape of exhaustion.

"There now," he said. "Do you want to tell me what frightened you? Was it a nightmare?"

"I don't think so. Sometimes I— I wake like this. I can't stop it. It's like a wave that drags me under and drowns me in dread."

"Why did you come out here?"

Why didn't you come to me?

"If I stay in the dark, it often won't relent, or it will plague me well into the morning. Sometimes I can distract myself out here until it goes away. The chill of the air, the busy garden chores, splashing my hands and face with cold water, burying my nose in lavender. I can focus my mind on other things, and eventually it passes. But…

this time it felt impossible." Her head lifted from his chest, and the night chill kissed his skin.

Skin. He'd not buttoned his shirt.

"You're better now?" he ventured. "Can you stand?"

Nodding, she allowed him to help her up, but when he would have pulled back, she stepped forward, keeping their bodies pressed together.

"Wait." She laid her cheek back against his heart, finding the rhythm with her ear. One arm slid around his torso to rest on the column of muscle next to his spine, and the other traced the blue tattoo of a sneering skull right below his clavicle. "I didn't know you looked like this." Her fingertips charted a course over his pectoral, finding other images in the sparse smattering of hair on his chest.

She'd be too kind to say it if she found him hideous to look at.

His body was an unsightly map of fearsome beasts, weathered ships, weapons, icons, and symbols of death. She shouldn't look, but damned if he didn't want her to discover every inch.

"What are you doing?" This time, it was *his* voice that trembled.

"I cannot say. I just... like the way you feel." The hand on his back tested the dips and swells of his muscle there, fanning across his expanse of smooth skin. "The way you look." Her slight fingers skipped over the sensitive protrusion of his nipple with a featherlight caress, leaving trails of fire in their wake. "The way you hold me."

"Felicity," he growled as she bumped her way down a few ribs, finding the bandage on his healing wound and tracing the outside.

"I hate that you were hurt because of me."

He hated that she might be in danger because of him. Hated himself for lying to her, and for the truths that would cause her pain.

Hated that there was a decent voice somewhere beneath his thundering desire— so faint and low— that told him to pull back. To button his shirt and take her to bed.

To *her* bed.

Alone.

Gooseflesh rose over his entire body as she angled back to look up at him, drawing her hand around his torso until both palms splayed against his chest.

His breath locked behind his ribs as he discovered things about himself he never knew before. Things he imagined other people did know by his age.

Because they'd been touched by other human beings.

The feel of her nails brushing his skin was possibly the sweetest sensation he'd yet experienced. He wanted more of it. He wanted to lean into a scratch like a needy hound. The place where his ribs winged into his back was ticklish. And the graze of his nipple could be felt as a jolt of pleasure in his cock.

Pleasant lessons were these. Blissful discoveries.

"Close your eyes," she whispered.

Now that was a particularly terrible idea. When she looked like a perfect angel, a halo of gold cast over her hair by the lone lamp. Her unblemished skin glowing in the dark like a beacon. Eyes bruised with smudges of exhaustion beneath, but glittering with something both dark and dazzling.

He didn't want to close his eyes, not when it would hide this vision from him.

"Please close your eyes?" she beseeched him. "I can't do this if you're looking, I'm not brave enough."

He shut his eyes, unable to deny her anything.

Trusting she wouldn't hurt him.

Fingers slid up his chest to the muscles beneath his neck and then around to feather through his hair and draw his head low.

A kiss, no more substantial than a cloud of mist, whispered against his lips.

He should stop this. Not here. Not now. Not when she was in such a vulnerable state and his entire body was just one raw nerve.

Begging to be touched. To be soothed. To be stroked and caressed and all of the things he'd never been before.

All of the things, he realized now, that a human needed to feel alive.

To feel… anything.

The revelation came in a flood of unwarranted emotion as she teased the curves of his mouth with little presses and plucks of her own. Nibbling at his top lip, licking the bottom one before retreating. Testing the scar at the corner with a dart of her tongue.

Growling, he ripped his mouth from hers and brushed her hands off his chest before he gave her his back and retreated toward the door.

The little pats of her bare feet on the flagstones told him she didn't allow his withdrawal. "Gareth? Did I do something wrong?"

"All of this was wrong," he remonstrated in a dark, guttural tone.

But nothing in this world ever felt so good.

His name was not Gareth, for one, and then the truths only became more destructive from there. "You should be the one with your eyes closed," he snarled. "You shouldn't go around kissing monsters."

"Oh no." She rushed around him, gripping his shoulders just as he'd done to hers before. "No, Gareth, you mustn't think that. You are *not* a monster It's the world that is monstrous." Her palms lifted to his jaw, cupping it on both sides. "You are… a marvel. Your presence has been a miracle to me. I don't know what I'd have done if you hadn't found me."

It was the trust in her eyes that tied him in knots. The

earnest glow on her features that laid him to absolute waste.

"Felicity, I am not— I'm nothing like you think. You haven't witnessed who I am or what I am capable of. You might imagine you have because you saw me end less than a handful of men in your defense, but I promise you. It's so much worse than that."

"How?" Her hold didn't let up as she held his face captive in her velvet grip. "Tell me."

"There is no point in confessing because there is no absolving me," he warned, encircling her wrists and pulling her palms away from his skin, deciding to give her what truths he could tell. "I cut out all of the soft parts of myself when I was very young. I had to, so I could be steel and stone rather than flesh and blood. I did it so I could perform the ghastly deeds required of me, but only at first. After so long, I began to enjoy violence. And a few years later, I'd gone past caring at all. I became bored with it. Cold and impenetrable. Unfeeling. Ruthless. I've hurt those who didn't deserve it. I've taken what didn't belong to me. I've exacted revenge much more excruciating than the actual insult. You can't begin to understand who I—"

"Look here." She tucked chilly fingers into his and he couldn't help but warm them. Using his acquiescence, she brought one of their joined hands to his chest, and spread his own fingers over his heart before covering it with her palm.

"You are not steel and stone. This is flesh and blood. Warmth and awareness. You are a man, not a machine. And though you are hard, I do not think you cut out your softness. Someone else tried to cut it out of you, but you did not let them. I think you buried it somewhere in there, where they could not find it. Perhaps where *you* cannot find it, and have convinced yourself it does not exist. But I believe you could uncover that softness and reclaim your good heart. Let it beat again."

Gabriel had to swallow twice before he could form words. His limbs had become paralyzed, his pulse erratic and strange. His head swam with a miasma of thoughts, desires, fears, and fantasies. "I don't know how..."

She brought his knuckles to her cheek and dragged the downy skin over them like an affectionate cat before pressing her lips to each scarred bone.

His chest pumped harder as he watched, a captive of her sincerity.

"I think you do." She flicked a gaze at him from beneath her lashes. "You are gentle with me..."

"I don't always want to be."

A shy curl of her lip was her astonishing response. "Maybe someday, you won't have to."

He pulled his hand from her grip. "Don't say things like that to me, woman."

"Why not?" Her lashes fluttered in confusion.

"Because there *isn't* a someday for us, you know that as well as I do."

"But... if there were a way?" She lost a bit of the courage and composure she'd been using to seduce him, and uncertainty clouded her eyes. A tooth bit into her lower lip.

Gabriel could feel her curling into herself, searching him for any signs of substantiation. "If you'd no past, and I'd no future, would you want me? *Do* you want me? Or... have I fabricated this connection between us by some twist of romantic girlish illusion?"

It was the dawning of that horrible thought in her eyes that was his final undoing. The visible worry that she stood before him unwanted, that propelled him forward.

Shoving his fingers into her hair, he cupped the sides of her head only to claim her quivering mouth with a possessive kiss.

He'd meant to soothe her doubts with words. To tell her he'd never found a woman on this earth more desirable. That he burned for the barest liberty, and never allowed himself to hope for even something as miraculous as a kiss.

Reaching up, she threaded her own fingers into the hair at his nape, leaving him with no barrier against the press of her body.

This.

It was the only word he could conjure, and it encompassed everything.

This mouth. *This* kiss. *This* woman.

His every nerve sparked to life, hungry to catalogue every point of contact.

Gabriel had no frame of reference, but he *knew*, beyond the shadow of a doubt, that no sustenance, be it God- or man-made, rivaled Felicity Goode in taste or texture. No woman could even hope to compare.

She was too pure for this world. Too soft. Too open. She cared too much and trusted too easily. To kiss her was to glimpse what heaven might be like. To taste her was to sample ambrosia.

And to have her hands roaming his bare skin?

He'd never been a religious man, but he'd found a new goddess to worship. Because someday, they'd all be nothing but dust and shadows, but his dust would have mingled with divinity for a moment.

For a kiss.

And that made him something more than any other man alive.

He made no decisions, had no plan of seduction or advancement, but suddenly he'd circled her waist with his hands and lifted her onto the closest workbench without breaking the fusion of their mouths.

Tongues glided together in a wet exploration of a mounting inferno charged with a powerful, intangible element. Something like captured lightning. Electric and wild and unruly.

Her knees parted, and he moved between them. Where he belonged.

Where he yearned to stay.

Charting the curve of her jaw with his mouth, he dragged a moist exploration down the swanlike column of her neck, only to bury his face in her fragrant hair. He inhaled deep as he laved and sucked and sampled the delicate flesh connecting her neck and shoulder.

Her raw, husky gasp of surprise rippled over his skin in a sensual abrasion of sound and submission.

The sound brought everything that made him both man and animal roaring to the surface.

It was only the curl of her fist in his shirt that kept him tethered to his humanity. Tenderness bloomed beneath the pulsating desire, tempering it. She trusted him. She wanted him.

She didn't fear him. Didn't think he was a monster.

That in itself was miraculous.

His hands fell to her nightdress with a moan of equal parts torment and titillation. He plotted a course he'd no map to, down the dramatic slope of her back into a narrow waist, and then flaring to hips widened by her posture, seated with open legs.

Christ, he'd yearned for so long.

A lifetime.

The scent of her, spices and sweetness, frayed what was left of his sanity.

And the feel of her nails scoring his scalp, then angling south to dip beneath the open collar of his shirt and nudge it down his shoulders, unraveled it completely.

His fingers fell upon the belt of her wrapper, releasing it so he could plunge his hands inside. Wishing his hands were steady, he smoothed them over the silk of her gown, down to the swell of her breasts. They each gasped as his knuckles grazed her nipples, pulling them impossibly tighter. He tested the insignificant weight of her breasts, marveling at the pliant abundance of flesh. Unwittingly, his lips followed the path his hands had forged, kissing over the fabric until his lips hovered above the twin protrusions.

He encircled the silk with his mouth, gently pressing the pebbled peak between his lips.

The resulting arch in her back, accompanied by her breathy sob, encouraged him onward. Both his languages deserted him as he felt the abrasion of the silk against the stubble on his jaw.

Fuck, but he wanted her naked. Exposed and open, draped in a bed of silks and satins and velvet and fur, rolling in every decadent sensation as their skin slid against one another.

As he slid inside of her.

Never had he been so hard. So out of his fucking mind with lust.

And yet, a reverence kept him from rending the gown from her body. Better she stay covered for now. That his first exploration should have boundaries.

Only when her legs opened wider, did he realize that his hands had fallen to her thighs. He'd been so focused on discovering her breasts… but now a different warmth beckoned.

Wanting to spare her the intensity of his visage, he couldn't help but straighten to gaze down on her. To gauge her reluctance or her acceptance. To observe her reactions and assess her needs, as he had no knowledge or skill to draw upon.

For once, he couldn't find a single hint of fear anywhere on her beautiful features.

Thank God.

It was the only thing that could have stopped him.

Both of his hands resting on her thighs, he used his thumbs to caress the quivering muscle beneath the gown, searching for the seam of undergarments.

He went as high on her thigh as he could, finding none.

No discovery ever made by a man had been so erotic. Of this, he was certain.

Their eyes locked as his thumb ventured forward, discovering the little thatch of soft hair against the silk.

Her mouth opened, but no sound escaped. Only increasingly short breaths.

How anyone could breathe at a time like this was beyond him.

Emboldened, he found the seam to her sex and ventured forward, sliding through the folds. The silk beneath the pad of his thumb became instantly damp and slick, and the whimper she emitted froze him in place.

He whispered her name. A plea. A prayer. A request for permission.

Her eyes were wide behind her spectacles, but she rolled her hips forward, pressing the sweet outline of her sex against his finger as she lifted her face in search of a reassuring kiss.

Barely able to focus on what his lips and fingers were doing in tandem, he closed his eyes and gave in to pure instinct. Delving with his tongue. With his thumb.

Until she let out a little cry into his mouth.

When he would have pulled back, her hand went to his, imprisoning him there.

There.

"There," she gasped. "*Oh.* Oh my."

The wondrous pleasure in her voice elicited a surge of masculine elation. He'd found something. Something she wanted. Something she liked. A turgid little nub just below the peak of her soft mound.

He thrummed it over the wet silk with the pad of his thumb. Once. Twice. Eliciting hitches of breath from her each time.

"Yes." She answered the question he didn't ask. "Yes. Like that. It… it feels like… like…"

Words seemed to abandon her as he dared to press a little deeper, to stroke a little faster. Her thighs twitched beneath his hands, clenching and releasing in demanding little bursts. She clutched at his shoulders and tossed back her head, exposing the vulnerable skin of her throat.

Unable to stop himself, he pressed his lips beneath her jaw and tasted the rich flavor of her skin. Soap and salt and something sweeter. Something undeniably Felicity.

In that moment, Gabriel knew he had to taste all of her before he would ever be satisfied.

Every inch.

He didn't know what he expected to find between her thighs, but these pleats of moist heat were better than anything his imagination conjured. To press his cock here, to locate the source of the wetness—

Felicity's fingers became gentle claws, scoring their way over the quivering ridges of his abdomen only to stop at the barrier of his waistband.

Every thought he had deserted him like a flock of scattered birds at the shot of a rifle.

She slipped a finger beneath his waistband, pulling his hips closer, drawing his body against hers as she arched up for another kiss.

Those curious, devious hands ventured down the placket of buttons, finding the turgid ridge of his sex aching to reach her.

At her first caress, his palms slammed to the shelf on both sides of her, holding the weight that his knees could no longer support.

"It's… so thick," she marveled in his ear.

Her testing of the length and girth of him only produced strangled, desperate sounds from his throat, as he fought not to unman himself right there.

"Am I hurting you?" she fretted.

He shook his head, and that seemed to embolden her to attempt to grip him.

"Christ. Jesus. *Fuck*."

He should be ashamed of his blasphemy in her presence, but it exploded from him in helpless bursts.

"What does it feel like?" Her hot breath was an erotic torment on his neck.

"There aren't... words."

"Not even one?" she pleaded.

He searched through the cavern of his mind, swimming through lust-addled thoughts. "Sharp but aching... throbbing. Needing..." His words dissolved into a breathless groan.

"I felt that too," she admitted shyly. "Is intimacy always like this? So powerful?"

"I— I don't—" His forehead fell to her shoulder. He couldn't take much more of this.

"May I touch you?" She fiddled with the placket of his trousers, releasing a few buttons, apparently confident of his reply. "Your skin? Your—"

"*God*, yes."

Her legs opened wider, and she released one hand from his trousers to pull the hem of her nightshift higher. "Will you touch me? As you did before?"

This couldn't be happening. It was like some sort of fantastical dream come to life.

His hand fell to her bare knee and inched higher, discovering the especially delicate skin on the inside of her slim thigh.

Just as Gabriel was about to start believing in God again, a carriage careened into the courtyard with a thunderous crash. It pulled to a stop next to the stables, just short of the greenhouse.

Gabriel jumped back, securing his trousers and shirt while she belted her wrapper, gritting out every foul word he knew.

He retrieved the pistol and gripped it with easy confidence, as he threw her nightshift over her knees, lifted her from the bench, and shoved her behind him.

From between rows of lush greenery, Gabriel watched a tall form leap out of the carriage, and he aimed at the center of the broad chest with the barrel of his gun.

He would happily shoot the interloper for the interruption alone.

To his surprise, the man reached back into the carriage to collect something.

Or someone.

Out stepped a woman dressed in a smart tweed traveling kit, her hair gleaming gold in the lanternlight of the coach.

A woman identical to the one behind him.

"Mercy!" Felicity lunged around him, threw open the doors of the glasshouse, and dashed for her rather astounded identical twin. "My God, you're here! You're really back!"

"Felicity!" Upon recognition, her twin's face crumbled as she picked up her skirt and ran forward. They collapsed, sobbing, against one another, speaking in strange, weeping gibberish not even the most talented of linguists could have deciphered.

Uncocking his pistol, Gabriel tucked it into the back of his trousers and finished buttoning his shirt to his throat, glad it was long enough to cover his deflating erection.

"What are you doing back?" Felicity asked, the sisters seeming unable to release each other, even as they levered away slightly to take in the identical image before them. "And at this hour? Is everything all right?"

Mercy squeezed her and planted a hasty kiss on her cheek. "I know we got in on the late train, but I simply couldn't stand to be away from you a moment longer. Besides, I received a letter from Morley stating that he'd made it safe for us to return and— Felicity, who is this?"

Mercy narrowed her eyes at Gabriel as he ducked out of the greenhouse, her quick mind making the correct assumptions that drew the corners of her lips lower and lower.

Felicity brightened, despite a blush creeping over her cheeks. "Oh, this is—"

"Gabriel?" Raphael's incredulous voice both elated and destroyed him.

His beloved brother had returned to him.

And because of that, it was all over.

Lean and satirically handsome, Raphael sported duskier skin and incrementally lighter hair than when he'd left. But that wasn't the most obvious change.

He seemed relaxed. Happy. It glowed from him as if even the dull English weather couldn't dim whatever sunlight he'd absorbed in paradise.

Because paradise traveled with him in the form of his wife.

"Gabriel, my God, it's you!" Raphael came to him in long strides, seizing him in a strong, backslapping hug. One he could do nothing but return. The assessment his brother gave his features filled him with trepidation.

"You look *incroyable*." His brother had been the only human who'd meant anything to him.

Until her.

"What is the matter, *mon frere*? You are not happy to see me?" Raphael nudged him. "Don't tell me you—"

"Gabriel?" Felicity pronounced his name— his real name— in the French accent his brother had used before she switched back to her own English translation of the word. "As in... Gabriel Sauvageau?"

A lump too large to swallow formed in his throat.

"What is my brother doing—?" Raphael turned to Felicity, and one glance at her expression wiped the smile from his lips and drew the color from his face.

Felicity answered no one, looking only at him. "Not... Gareth Severand?"

As if aware he'd stepped into a pile of excrement while wearing the wrong shoe, Raphael quickly did his best to cover his tracks. "Well, we've the papers, *n'est-ce pas*? New identities to keep the police and our enemies unaware of our existence. I'm Remy Severand, for example."

"You still didn't know?" Mercy's mouth dropped open.

"I didn't recognize him..." Felicity adjusted her spectacles, staring at him as if he'd become a stranger.

Or a monster.

"Well, look, he's almost handsome now." Raphael gripped both of his shoulders, standing before him to study the work he'd had done. "Christ, man, that Titus Conleith is a bloody genius."

"Titus did this?" Felicity's voice climbed an octave higher and a decibel louder. "He— he told me you had *died*. That you'd been shot saving me."

"I know." The condemnation in her eyes felt like a nail in Gabriel's coffin. One he was ready to craft right now and climb into, just to avoid that look of betrayal. "And every word Titus told you was the truth. He simply... omitted that I'd survived the ordeal."

Mercy clutched her tighter. "Morley decided it was safer, darling, the fewer people who knew about Gabriel's survival, for the time being. And when the information was deemed safe, our parents had that dreadful accident and everything was chaos. Right after that settled somewhat, Nora broke the news of her pregnancy and... well... Gabriel was supposed to have left the country by now." She shot him a withering glare. "None of us knew his existence would mean a jot to you, nor that you would end up so scantily clad with him in the middle of the night."

Felicity wrenched away from her sister, her fists balled tight and her face breaking out in a bloom of angry red. "I was the *only* one of you who didn't know? You—my own twin sister! My closest confidant. You kept it from me?"

"Only to protect you," Gabriel blurted, suddenly able to crawl out of the tar pit of guilt that'd nearly dragged him under.

She whirled on him. "I don't need *protection*."

He pressed his lips closed, knowing that now wasn't the time to disagree.

Her expression flattened as she crossed her arms over her chest. "I realize I hired you for your protection *physically*. But I don't need to be protected *from information*, is what I meant."

"But, Felicity." Mercy stepped forward, her hands reaching out in a penitent gesture. "You'd just been through something so traumatizing. The fire at the Midnight Masquerade. Being shot at, kidnapped, and attacked. The subsequent head wound. We didn't want to burden your delicate constitution with anything that might add to your fear."

Gabriel wished she'd yell. That she'd lose her temper and throw things, berate and abuse them; it was what he deserved. Instead, her shoulders sagged and bitter tears sprang to her eyes.

"I *know* I am always afraid," she said in a voice all the more devastating for its softness. "But that doesn't mean I cannot be brave. I fear the unknown most of all. It is a cruelty to keep me in the dark. I thought you knew that, Mercy."

She whirled away from her sister before she had to endure an explanation or an apology, pinning Gabriel with her pain.

"I— I mourned you." She shook her head as if she couldn't believe it. "I planted a flower for you in there, and tended it in your name. What a gullible, infantile fool you must think I am. A complete idiot."

He stepped forward. "Felicity, I—"

"How did I not know? Where is your accent?"

Deflating, he decided that from there on out, he'd never again tell her a lie. "I practiced an English accent while I was recovering from all the surgeries... I couldn't sound like myself if my identity were to change."

She nodded as if she understood, though the look of pure misery threatened to crush him into the dirt before she covered her face with her hands in mortification. "We would have... You were going to... And I didn't even know your real name."

"Felicity..." He reached for her, but she shrank away.

"I can't look at you. At *any* of you..." She shoved past him, fleeing into the house.

All three of them flinched as the door clicked shut. She'd not even slammed it. It wasn't her way.

Something inside of Gabriel hollowed out. His life had been a slog through so much gore and horror and inhumanity. People had been afraid of him, spat at him, humiliated and reviled him.

But not until today had he ever felt small.

Raphael stepped up to stand shoulder to shoulder with him. "What are you doing here, Gabriel? With her?"

Mercy marched around to face them both, looking like a furious school mistress. "Are you lovers?" she demanded, her eyes sweeping over his state of *dishabille*.

Gabriel was not in the habit of explaining himself, but in this case, he knew one was owed. "We are not lovers."

"That's not what it looks like."

"We kissed, that is all."

"What did she mean about protection?"

Right, her letter would not have reached them in Iceland, if they'd decided to sail home.

"Someone left a threatening letter in the house, and

she was accosted in the streets a few weeks ago, so she hired me— well, Gareth Severand— as a personal guard."

"Who accosted her?" Increasingly distressed, Mercy paced this way and that. "Who sent the letter? What did it say? No one knew of this!"

Gabriel sprang to her defense. "She wrote to Reykjavík to tell you. But Sir and Lady Morley were in France, and she didn't want to visit her troubles on Conleith and his wife, who I understand is suffering a difficult pregnancy. So, while she was left to her own devices by her family, to select a husband from the twats in the *ton*, she put an advertisement in the paper through a security service."

"And you answered it?" Raphael asked quietly, understanding dawning in his eyes. "To protect her."

Gabriel dragged a hand over his tense features. "I was — in the neighborhood and she assumed I was one of the applicants. She hired me on sight, but she did not recognize me. I… thought it would be safer if I did not divulge my identity."

"Safer for whom, exactly?" Mercy snapped.

"My plan was to leave when I— removed the threat, and she'd be none the wiser." He sent Raphael a grave look. "We were attacked last week at a ball. I… I fought Honeycutt and Smythe."

"You gutted them, I hope." Mercy sliced right through his attempt at discretion for her sake.

"I crushed them, and we were long gone before questions were asked. No one would even look in Felicity's direction."

"You don't think Marco is sending old Fauves after you?" Raphael queried.

"I don't see how." Gabriel blew out a breath. "But I've been wondering the same thing. If he didn't before, he might now, as I've made a few inquiries. I refuse to sit and wait for the next attack. I'll bring the war to him, if that is the case."

Raphael shook his head, squeezing at tension in the back of his neck. "How would Marco Villanueve even know we're alive, let alone that you've been watching Felicity?"

"What do you mean watching her?" Mercy's eyes narrowed on her husband, then turned on Gabriel, flaring with temper. "In the area, were you? Have you had designs on Felicity all this time? Have you been lurking about, waiting for the chance to swoop in on her affections and seduce a sweet, vulnerable, romantic girl who is obviously much too young for you—"

"Mercy..." Raphael caught her hand and brought it to his lips. "Please."

"No, no!" She snatched her hand back and shook a furious fist at both of them as they stood before her diminutive frame like enormous, scolded boys. "Felicity knows nothing of men but what she reads in those damned books, aside from our overbearing father, who made her feel like her very existence was a mistake. He belittled and berated her because of her clumsiness as a child. And when it was discovered she was good as blind, we all sheltered her because she couldn't see when danger was coming at her. She'd never see *you* coming for her until you owned her gentle heart. You were her first kiss, I hope you realize. The first man she let into this house alone. And you deceived her. A woman's heart doesn't forget that."

"I know." Gabriel stood and let her truth batter against him. It was what he deserved, what he'd wished Felicity had said and done.

"I'm going to go check on her," she announced.

Her husband reached for her hand and gave her a gentle tug before she could storm away. "Let me, *mon chaton*?"

"Why would I? You're a *man*. Don't think that this isn't somehow also your fault." She waggled a finger at him.

"It's all of our faults..." Gabriel muttered, seizing their attention. "Felicity is right, you know. We never should have lied to her. I thought to protect her, but I realize that was a high-handed, devious, self-serving thing to do."

"Mercy," Raphael said with a bit more fervency this time. "My brother never had *designs* on your sister, he had *feelings* for her. Always. Since the night we all met."

Mercy's mouth clamped shut. Fell open. Then shut again. She blinked at him as if she needed a moment to reassess her view of the entire situation.

Raphael's knuckles grazed his wife's jaw. "Please, darling. Go get comfortable and cleaned up from your travels and allow me to talk to your sister. Trust me. I know a thing or two about calming a distraught Goode girl."

She snorted, but relented. "If you upset her further or make her cry, I'll hang you both by your bootstraps and decapitate anyone who dares try to cut you down."

Raphael watched as Mercy marched to the ornate courtyard entrance, her skirt swishing in angry little motions behind her. "I adore her vicious threats. She'd have made an excellent crime lord, don't you think?"

Gabriel let out a low whistle of agreement. "She'd have been the most ruthless the underworld has yet seen."

"Do not worry, *mon frere*." Raphael put his hand on Gabriel's shoulder, and the weight comforted him mightily. "We will put this to rights."

"I should go to her," Gabriel said. "It's my apology she deserves first and foremost. She should take anger out on me."

"Gabriel." His brother turned to him, searched his face as if he still couldn't believe it. "I have some things to say to her that need to be said. The woman said she did not want to see you, and… at least for tonight, I think you should respect that."

Gabriel nodded. "You're right."

"Get a drink, yes? You look like you need one." Raphael sauntered into the house with his signature loose-limbed confidence, leaving him alone.

An abysmal shame and agony welled up from so deep within, Gabriel whirled and put his fist through one of the panes of the greenhouse, shattering it beneath the blow.

Feeling only nominally better, he inspected the damage to his fist, which was astonishingly minimal. Only a few small cuts and barely a drop of blood. He stretched the skin with a curl of his fingers, testing it, ripping it further. Needing some sort of pain to ground him back into his body.

This was why he didn't belong with Felicity Goode. Because she wanted a gentle palm in which to place her tender heart.

And he only knew how to make a fist.

CHAPTER 13

Felicity paced the room, shaking with every elemental emotion. First with the hot lance of anger, then with the whirlwind of shame for that anger. Thereafter, the scorched earth was flooded by hurt and then buried beneath humiliation.

Was there ever a woman who didn't have to claw her way through a graveyard of shame?

She hadn't even done anything, and yet here it was.

It was merely that… the look in his gunmetal eyes had been enough to melt her.

Because she glimpsed the shame there, too.

It was humiliation at the base of her ire. Her family thought her nothing more than a child, one to be coddled and cosseted. Lied to.

For her own protection.

Because she didn't have the emotional fortitude to handle hard and frightening truths.

They weren't wrong. That was the worst of it. Terror overwhelmed her sometimes, dread and doubt overtook her sense of practicality until she was certain the world would stop spinning at any moment.

It was why she escaped into her romantic fantasies. Because she had to remind herself that there were happy endings, even in those moments when her mind told her such a thing was impossible.

Because she knew that they occurred; she'd watched it happen to her sisters with no small amount of envy.

And she thought…

Well, it didn't bear consideration. It was always impossible. The massive, menacing stranger who protected her had teased those fantasies out of her imagination, and there were moments when she'd hoped that… that they might find a way.

And because she was so naïve, so inexperienced and sheltered, it'd never occurred to her that he was a man who'd deceived his way into her home.

Into her heart.

The decisive knock on her door came as no surprise.

"Come in, Mercy," she sighed.

Her door creaked open, and Raphael's dark head peeked around the edge. "It isn't Mercy, but would you allow me to speak with you for a moment?"

Felicity took a moment to study him. Though there wasn't more than two years' difference in age between Gabriel and his brother, Raphael had the appearance of someone much younger. Even without the scars, Gabriel wouldn't have been as effortlessly handsome as his brother. Whereas Gabriel's features were brutal and striking, Raphael might as well have been the arch angel he'd been named for. A glimmer of mischief in his hazel eyes, and a charm and confidence only the devil himself might possess, made for a potently compelling combination.

No wonder Mercy had fallen for him so quickly. They must endlessly challenge and entertain each other.

Felicity didn't know this man. But she ought to. And, technically, he'd done nothing to wrong her.

"Very well, come in." She motioned to a pair of high-backed arabesque chairs drawn close to the fireplace.

He took one seat, and she perched on the one opposite him.

Leaning forward, his features set in an intent and earnest expression of concern. "Let me assure you, I'm not here to talk you out of being angry with Gabriel..."

Felicity stared into the fire. "I'm angrier at myself than anything."

"No, dear Felicity, there is no cause for that—"

"I've met the man twice, how did I not recognize him?" she asked bitterly. "His size alone is tremendously unique."

"But not unheard of. You said yourself, you were allowed to believe he was dead. And surely you recall how he looked before... little more than scars clinging to a misshapen skull. His nose completely gone, his eyelid dropping so low he could barely open it. That macabre half-smile of a scar. He had to keep his hair shorn so his mask didn't tug at it and give him terrible headaches. Now, he has a better mane than even me."

She'd reveled in the feel of his hair sifting through her fingers.

"It will take time even for me to get used to him," Raphael confided. "He doesn't look like he did before the — his injuries. So do not punish yourself for not seeing him for who he is."

"You are kind," she replied gratefully. "But that doesn't change the fact that I'm so dreadfully gullible. So blind and eager. There is something very wrong with me if my entire family, including *him,* thought I was too stupid or too weak to know the truth."

Raphael sat back against the chair, plunking his head against the headrest with a rueful sigh. "I agree that keeping things from you was wrong of everyone. I would be furious in your position, because, though everyone's intentions were based in love, it did rather denote a lack of respect. And that, in my world, is the greatest insult.

Especially when you are a woman who deserves that regard."

His validation did a great deal to cool her tempestuous emotions.

"After the Masquerade, everyone wanted you to remain untouched by my— and by extension Gabriel's— intrusion into the family. Especially since it had no immediate effect on you because we were both supposed to be across the entire globe from each other. And you had so many things here to worry about." He huffed out a sound of sardonic wonder. "I knew that Gabriel... that he was drawn to you. But I will say that no one in the world, including me, could have predicted that he would approach you. That he would take this position..."

"He didn't," she admitted, plucking at a stray bit of lace on her wrapper. "Not really. Now that I think about it, I rather wrangled him inside and offered him the job without even asking for references." Standing, she reached for the poker and stabbed at the fire. "I am a fool. He told me as much that day. I deserve everyone's derision."

"Why did you hire him? This large, scarred, obviously malevolent man, devoid of charm or a pretty vocabulary, let alone a face that is a pleasure to look at."

"You're being cruel to him."

"I'm being honest. And I'm asking you to do the same." His words were sharp, stabbing like barbs into her back. "Do you love him?"

She jabbed rather viciously at a glowing white log, sending sparks showering up the chimney. "How can I answer that? I don't know him."

"But you know how you feel," he pressed.

She searched her heart, which beat like the wings of a trapped bird refusing to land. "Right now, I feel a little bit of everything, and cannot identify one particular emotion."

"That is fair enough."

At that, she turned back and reclaimed the edge of her seat. "Why did you come here?" she asked, sensing his reluctance. "If it wasn't to plead your brother's or your wife's case?"

The look he gave her was one of approval. "Do you know what happened to my brother? Why he looked the way he did— the way he does?"

Struck by the memory of his pitiable face, she closed her eyes against a well of sorrow. "He said he was protecting someone."

"Me." The word was a low lamentation. "He was protecting me. Gabriel was always so large, so fiendishly strong. When my father needed money, he put Gabriel into the fighting pits and bet on him."

Felicity gripped the arm of the chair, never once considering their story could be so contemptable.

"One time," Raphael's gaze became unfocused as he looked into the past, "my father put me in the ring, and then bet that I would lose. I was a small lad. I could fight, but I hadn't the brute strength or killer instinct Gabriel had developed. Upon learning of this, Gabriel locked me in a trunk and took my place in the pit. That night, someone hit Gabriel with a plank of heavy wood, and tore his nose clean off. It would have crushed me. I was all but thirteen. He was fifteen."

A tear fell for the boys before she even knew it had welled within.

"And after, he still fought in the ring as a freak they dubbed the Monster of Monaco. Once my father founded the Fauves, he relieved Gabriel of the pits, but he then groomed us to be gangsters. We extorted people out of money, we beat them to keep them in line. We were beasts. We *are* beasts; I am merely a more elegant creature than he is."

"Why are you telling me this?" Felicity dashed at her

damp cheeks. "In hopes that I'll forgive him? That I'll pity him?"

Because it was working. Her heart was an open wound. Everything he'd said before made perfect sense. He'd been trying to warn her all along.

And she'd been too besotted to listen.

Raphael reached to her and took her hand. His hold reminded her of Morley's or Titus's. Gentle. Platonic.

But his had a deeper, more fervent zeal behind it. "You have a soft heart, Felicity Goode. And in *your* world, that is an admirable quality. Gabriel, he… he has powerful feelings for you… he has since that first moment we met by the sea. And even though you are angry or hurt, I want you to trust the fact that he will die to keep you from harm. That is how we are."

Felicity nodded and squeezed his hand. "I believe that," she murmured.

"I will leave you with this one thought," he said as his grip strengthened. "Though he will protect you, Gabriel is no shield, *mon sœur*. He was raised, conditioned, to be a weapon. We have a saying where I come from: You might use a spear as a cane, but that doesn't change its destiny."

"Are you warning me away from him?" Felicity put a hand to her throat.

"I'm saying that I'm not certain Gabriel knows how to do anything *but* hurt people. It's all he ever knew. All he was ever good at. He's never had a pet, let alone a lover. I don't know if he's divulged that to you. If you'll excuse my forwardness, I feel you must know. It isn't that he hasn't lain with a woman, it's that he's never kissed one, touched, flirted with… nothing." He glanced down, fighting an obvious battle within himself, as she knew he must feel as though he were breaking some sort of confidence. "I thought he never touched a woman because of how he looked, but I'm not sure that's it, entirely…"

"What do you think it is?" she breathed.

"He never learned how to handle fragile things without breaking them. I think that frightens him." Raphael asked the question as if he didn't want the answer. "Has he... has he ever frightened you?"

"Not once," she said with ardent meaning. "I've always known I'm safe at his side, and have never needed safety *from* him. That's just it..." She looked up, her eyes threatening to spill over again. "He tells me all the time he is not kind. Insists he is every sort of terrible and treacherous thing... but he's never been anything but gentle with me."

Raphael's own features tightened with emotion.

"Because we no longer wanted to be criminals, it turned some of our men into enemies. Marco, the one who struck you, it was not confirmed that he died in the fire. We are afraid he's behind your current need for protection. That it is Gabriel's feelings for you that put you in danger in the first place. I don't think you can imagine the guilt he carries for that."

She digested that information for a moment, shredded to bits by claws of ragged grief for what her terse protector had been through. "If only I'd have known..."

Raphael nodded. "I agree. You should have known. But Gabriel's protection of you was unfortunately absolute. I know my brother. He would spare you having to carry a secret. Or the fear such an enemy might impose upon you, especially when fear already seems to be your particular foe. He knows so little about women; he doesn't realize that creatures so delicate can also demonstrate such immense strength. His greatest sin is that he underestimated you, but I feel it was done in ignorance, not condescension."

Felicity covered her eyes. Wishing like hell she could be different somehow. That she could have inherited only a modicum of Mercy's boldness, Prudence's sense of adventure, or Honoria's courage.

A crack of thunder ignited her frayed nerves, causing

her to jump, just before the sky opened up to release a torrent of rain.

Raphael put his hands on his thighs and pushed to his feet. "It is late. Perhaps we should rest and talk about this in the morning?"

"Actually, I need to speak with Mercy. I've much to tell her."

He nodded. "I hope you forgive Mercy. She hated the idea from the start. It would break her heart if there were a chasm between you."

She nodded, loving him a little for his regard of her sister.

"Raphael? I'm glad you've both come home."

His features softened into a lovely smile. "So am I, *mon sœur.*"

She took his arm and he conducted her down the hall with all the ceremony of someone escorting a queen to court. When they passed Gabriel's door, she hesitated but somehow knew she wouldn't find him skulking in his room. That wasn't his way.

Mercy met them on the stairs, her features anxious and expectant. "Felicity, I—"

"It's all right." She embraced her sister. "I'm not angry any longer."

"Oh good." Mercy squeezed a little too hard. "You know I hate apologizing. I've never been good at it."

Suddenly she was so glad to have her sister back, she couldn't decide whether to giggle or cry.

"Where *is* everyone?" Mercy asked, keeping one arm locked around her as they made their way to the parlor. "I can't even find Mrs. Winterton."

Felicity revealed the entire story of the letter, the poison ingested by Mrs. Winterton, her attack in the street that led her to posting the advertisement for a guard. She told them of the fight in the garden, and didn't miss the meaningful glance between Mercy and Raphael as she recounted Gabriel's bravery that night.

After careful thought, she omitted the part about her fainting.

"Where is Gabriel?" Raphael queried. "I was certain he'd be prowling close by."

Mercy shrugged. "He was patching a broken windowpane with planks on the glasshouse, last I saw."

Raphael nodded, tapping his chin in a pensive posture. "I will consult with him, but the poisoning aspect of this... it doesn't feel like Marco. Neither does hiring others to do his wet work. If there is killing to be done, that bastard will jump at the chance to get his hands dirty every time." He studied Felicity so intently, she swore she could hear the gears of his brain grinding away. "Tell me of this fortune you have inherited... It is common knowledge?"

Felicity squirmed. "Yes."

"Have you turned down any proposals lately, from men who would be after your assets?"

"There have been a several suitors of interest, most recently the Earl of Bainbridge. However, he proposed *after* I was threatened or attacked. I can't think of what his motive would be."

"I can," Mercy interjected. "He is our cousin of some distance, and an earl, besides, but I have heard he's quite penniless. He needs an heiress."

"Yes, but he was honest with me about that. It's part of why I decided we wouldn't suit. And while he made it abundantly clear that he didn't love me, he was nothing but cordial when I refused him."

Raphael stroked his angular jaw. "Bainbridge... he lives in the vicinity?"

"He does, just on the other side of the park."

Nodding, he seemed to come to a conclusion. "Well, it's important we find Marco whether he's behind this or not. I won't feel that either of you are safe until I'm able to spit on his grave. However, I'd like to speak to this Bainbridge."

"Gareth— Gabriel didn't seem to think highly of him," she said.

Smirking, Raphael went to the door. "My brother has excellent instincts, though in this case, they might be a bit suspect. Perhaps we can get Morley involved, now that he's back from the Continent."

At that, Felicity groaned. "I don't want everyone to make a fuss."

"If your life is in danger, Felicity," Mercy shook her elbow, "best you get used to a bit of fuss, and be glad it's not an all-out war."

Felicity proffered a weak smile, deeply grateful for such a family as this, regardless of her trepidation over the attention.

"Well, let us all get some much-needed rest, yes?" Raphael yawned, though whether in earnest or for effect, it was difficult to say.

Felicity stood and kissed her sister goodnight, reveling in their closeness, as if one half of her had been returned. "I missed you. I'm glad you're back."

"I made it back just in time, I see," Mercy said, clinging to her. "I'll go to hell before I see you married for anything but affection. I don't care what Father wrote in that damned will. He was wrong. It was like a parting shot."

At that, Felicity tensed. "Does my fortune go to Bainbridge upon my death?"

"No," Mercy answered.

"Then, who?"

Her sister's mouth fell open. "The solicitor said there was a list of names, but he cannot reveal them to you or to the other recipients until such time as is deemed necessary."

"Say someone found out..." Felicity postulated. "Shouldn't everyone on that list be considered a suspect?"

"Then it is the solicitor we go to first thing," Raphael said, his eyes glittering with a dark anticipation. "We'll *make* him talk."

CHAPTER 14

Knowing sleep was impossible, Felicity stood outside Gabriel's door for several breaths.

She could feel him in there. A man like that carried some sort of atmosphere with him, like the current in the air before a storm broke.

A warning, most probably, to creatures of prey.

The effects of his nearness were familiar to her now. Little vibrations of the fine hairs on her body or a prickle of awareness washing down her spine.

Except the thought of him devouring her made her tremble with emotions other than fear.

I am not kind.

He'd said that to her in the very beginning. He'd always cautioned her about who he was. And yet, it was in his very sin against her that he proved his own claim false.

His lie was meant to be kind.

Lifting her fist, she meant to knock at his door. But froze.

Asking for what she wanted, what she needed, had rarely ever gone well, and Raphael's revelations about his brother had both clarified and complicated things.

She'd been shattered by discovery of his past. By the

barbarity he'd had to endure. And she did comprehend that his hands knew no other trade than violence and crime.

He'd never had a woman. Never been a lover.

Never been loved.

He was a weapon, and she was nothing of the sort.

Everything said and left unsaid between them surged from her breath and broke on the barrier of the door. What would this conversation look like? When they were both so overwrought and frustrated by everything from desire to circumstance. Would he be kind, now that the lie was uncovered?

Would he stay?

She lowered her hand back to her side, calling herself nine shades of coward.

Not tonight. If things went terribly between them, she'd not have the fortitude to withstand his rejection or abandonment.

With a frustrated sigh, she slunk away to the stairs, heading down toward her father's study across from her parlor in the front hall.

There, in the extraordinarily masculine space, she used her lamplight to search through what little paperwork had been left in his enormous desk, deemed personal by the solicitors and accountants. If they'd not found anything of note in the more official documents, perhaps she could find a clue in the personal effects she hadn't yet gotten around to sorting out.

After more than an hour of reading records with financial or legal language she barely comprehended, she slid off her spectacles and rubbed at her tired eyes. All she had left were the household accounts. Opening that book, she squinted down at the tedious figures beneath her, written in her father's decisive script.

Here was his life in integers. In money, the thing he'd valued over his own family.

With a wistful sort of resentment, she ran her fingers over the long sheet. Past payments for stable feed and servants' salaries going back years. She found where he installed the broiler that now heated their running hot water, and her eyes bulged at the expense. She found her sisters' allowances, and where they stopped when they'd each taken husbands without his consent.

But what was this? Quarterly payments by banknote to an M.W. Goode at Fairhaven House, in a staggering amount.

If Felicity had yearned for anything in her life, it'd been extended family.

Her parents were both only children, so far as she knew, and neither of them had come from prolific stock. Had her father been helping some distant relative? Someone far more removed than even Bainbridge?

Encouraged, she frantically went through several files, coming up with nothing. On a whim, she searched through all the drawers, shelves, and even his cigar box, finding them infuriatingly empty.

Blowing out a faint curse on a frustrated breath, his bookshelf caught her eye.

Of course. The family Bible. Her father had been a zealous man, perhaps M.W. Goode would be mentioned in the records of family births and deaths.

She lifted it down, turning through centuries of names with no little amount of awe, finding no one with those particular initials.

But an edge caught her attention, the outline of thick paper snared beneath the thin pages of gold-leafed scripture.

Extracting it, she unfolded what happened to be a deed to an estate.

Fairhaven House.

Apparently, a modest manor with acreage on some benighted moor in the north. She could find no income from agriculture or tenants, which wasn't at all like her father...

So who was this M.W. Goode?

Heavy boots landed at the bottom of the grand staircase and angled back toward the courtyard.

Only one man in this household walked with that rhythm.

And he was going out into the storm.

Felicity abandoned her discovery as she dashed out the study and down the hall after Gabriel, her bare feet flying over the chilly marble floor.

He was already halfway across the courtyard when she reached the threshold and threw open the door. "Gabriel, wait!" she called after him, gripping the frame and blinking against the mist blown in from the deluge, dotting her spectacles.

He froze, massive shoulders hunched beneath the upturned collar of his coat. His fists remained locked in his pockets, and he made no move to face her.

"Where are you going?"

His chin touched his shoulder, revealing the strong profile of his visage. "I'm going to find Marco... or perhaps that solicitor, I haven't decided yet."

"In the middle of the night? In this storm? It's ludicrous."

"It's the best time to scare the truth out of someone... or get rid of a body."

She held out a hand he couldn't see, stepping forward beneath the eaves. "Don't do that," she entreated. "The solicitor was only doing his job."

"And I'm doing mine, the one you hired me for."

"*No*. This is *not* what our contract entailed."

"Our agreement is that I keep you safe," he said over his shoulder before resuming his march toward the stables.

"Then stay *here* and protect me!" she demanded in an authoritative voice she didn't quite recognize as her own.

He ignored her.

"Please, Gabriel," she resulted to begging. "Come inside. Wait until the storm passes, at least. You'll catch your death. You must be freezing."

"No!" He whirled on her with such fury, she took a retreating step back into the house. Even from here, she could see his eyes were no longer grey, but molten quicksilver, snapping with unrestrained emotion.

"No, dammit," he snarled. "I'm not cold. I'm on *fire*. Do you understand? I have to escape this fucking house before I burn alive. Do you really expect me to sleep with only a wall separating us after—" The words died beneath a clash of thunder, but they each glanced toward the hothouse.

He stood like a warrior before an advancing army, rather than a man against a much smaller, unarmed woman. Feet planted, fists and jaw clenched, nostrils flaring. Rain sluicing down the grooves and scars of his savage face like the tears of an angry god.

Say something, Felicity ordered herself. *Say something. Don't be a coward.*

For some terrible reason, her jaw had locked shut.

He deflated with one endless breath, lifting a hand to slick back the wet gathers of his hair. "Felicity… I was wrong to deceive you. I'm just… so damned sorry. Your family is here now, and Raphael will keep you safe while I hunt for the threat on your life. It is time— it's *better*— that I go—"

"I'm on fire too." The words tripped from her mouth and fell into the gathering puddle between them.

He didn't blink. He didn't breathe.

And to her ultimate relief, he didn't leave.

"I'm on fire too," she repeated, more breathlessly this

time, as the visible vapor produced by the heat of her words reached out to him. "I… I want what you want."

He took one threatening step toward her, jabbing a finger in her direction. "You can't even *imagine* what I want."

She stepped down again, on the thin line of dry cobbles beneath the eaves. "What if I could?"

"Don't." He swiped a hand in the air as if to erase the sight of her. "Don't follow me." He turned and strode into the shadows between the courtyard gas lamps.

In what might have been her first impulsive decision of her lifetime, Felicity plunged into the frigid downpour and ran to catch up with him.

Seizing his arm with both hands, she spun him back to face her. "I'm not letting you leave like this," she cried over the storm. "What if I never see you again?"

Something in the grim set of his jaw told her that's exactly what he had in mind.

"Goddammit, Felicity, get inside where it's warm."

The rain drenched her almost immediately, gathering her hair into soaking strings. Plastering her nightgown and wrapper to her skin.

The drops stung, but she barely felt the pain.

"Come with me," she tugged again.

His gaze dropped to her body for only a moment as she stood blinking against the drops that ran down the surface of her spectacles, obscuring some of his expression from her view.

Swearing in his native language, he shrugged her away, only to rip his coat down his shoulders and thrust it around hers. It engulfed so much of her, it might as well have been a cloak.

"It's not safe." He jerked away once she was swaddled. "Don't you understand? Thirty years. *Thirty years* I've never— I'm simply not meant for a girl like you."

"*Woman,*" Felicity corrected. "I'm a *woman.* I want you

to acknowledge that, Gabriel Sauvageau. I am a woman, and just because I'm innocent does not mean that I am incapable of desire. Of understanding and expressing it just as well or better than you."

She swallowed as a familiar shy mortification crept into her cheeks, and she fought the instinct that screamed for her to sink into the coat and disappear.

No more.

She was tired of being invisible. Insignificant. Silent. If she didn't say her piece now, she might never get another chance. "I— I think about you often. In that way. All the time, in fact. And... when I'm in a room with you, I can look at no other man. For none compare."

She ventured forward on feet threatening to go numb, encouraged by the answering color of his own drenched skin. "When other men gleam brilliantly in the light, I look for you in the shadows. I yearn to join you there. Because you are beautiful."

He whirled away from her, giving every indication of a stallion about to bolt.

Rushing around him, she reached up and cupped either side of his jaw in her hands. Forcing him to face her, extraordinarily aware that he could toss her aside and disappear into the night should he take it in his mind to do so.

It didn't matter, she had to bare her heart to him or she'd never forgive herself.

"I am not being kind," she insisted, reading the admonishment in his eyes. "To me, you are the only creature worth looking at. Yours is the only body I want to discover. The only touch I've ever truly desired."

His nostrils flared.

His jaw flexed and shifted beneath her hands, and his entire enormous frame shook as he stared over her shoulder at the door to Cresthaven.

"I'm not like them," he spoke in a tight whisper, barely

audible over the rain. "I'm not like the men in your books."

"You are better," she insisted, caressing at his scars with the tender pad of her thumb. "You are real."

Finally becoming a casualty to the cold, she shifted on her bare feet, the numbness giving way to pain as a violent shiver overtook her.

He blinked down at her feet, then with several dark and foul curses, he swept her into his arms and carried her inside. He didn't stop until he'd climbed all three flights of stairs and shouldered into her bedroom.

Appointed in white and gold, the only other color in the room was that of the massive blue Persian rug in front of the fireplace. Gabriel took her there in three long strides, and she slid down his body as he set her on her feet before the roaring fire.

It was like standing on a bed of pins and needles at first, and she gritted her teeth against chattering as he disappeared into the adjoining washroom.

Working quickly, Felicity dashed the down coverlet from her bed and settled it before the fire. Then she shrugged out of his coat, peeled away her sopping wrapper and grappled with the buttons of her nightshift, struggling to tug it over her head in time to discard it before he returned.

Naked, she turned and bent to stretch them on the warm stones of the hearth.

Mrs. Pickering wouldn't likely get to the wash soon, what with her maids gone, and she shouldn't want them to go sour in the laundry basket.

"Jesus *fucking* Christ."

The blasphemy was spoken like a prayer, and Felicity straightened and turned to find Gabriel in her doorframe, his eyes peeled wide in abject disbelief and two clean bath towels pooled at his feet where he'd dropped them.

Still shivering, she stood as close as she dared to the

fire, her hands tucked under her chin and one knee bent in modesty she was trying not to feel whilst attempting a seduction.

"How thoughtful of you," she prompted, offering him a shy smile.

"Wha'? Oh." He opened his hands as if surprised not to find the towels gripped there, and didn't peel his gaze from her as he bent his knees and groped at the floor for the discarded offerings. Approaching her like he would a dangerous animal, he offered her one from as far a distance as his arm span would allow.

When she took it, he retreated back to the door. "You don't know what you're doing," he warned, valiantly trying, and failing, to avert his eyes.

"You're right," she admitted as she took the towel and ran it down her shoulders and arms, her breasts, her belly, her thighs.

His gaze followed her motions, his tongue moistening his lips as he drank in the sight of her with an odd expression of disbelief. Like a man who'd been walking for days in the desert and didn't believe the oasis in front of him to be anything other than a mirage.

Unused to such a vulnerable silence, Felicity cleared a gather of nerves from her throat. "You see, I haven't the first idea what I'm doing, but… I was hoping, if you were to see me like this, you'd forget all the reasons you shouldn't make love to me."

He blinked. Twice.

A muscle in his hand twitched. As did one in his neck.

Then he was simultaneously advancing upon her and rending both his shirt and vest down the front.

Buttons made little plinking noises as they scattered across the floor in chaotic directions. He peeled the sleeves from his shoulders and abandoned the wet shirt to the carpet.

Before she could take in a proper look at him, he'd engulfed her in his arms and claimed her mouth with a kiss more primal and potent than any described in the written word thus far.

He besieged her with his lust, thrusting his tongue past the barrier of her lips with a wet, demanding glide. Caressing and tasting, he explored the recesses of her mouth in deep, drugging strokes.

The top layer of his skin was still damp and chilled, but the inferno beneath threatened to immolate her in the conflagration of his unsatisfied lust.

She would be a willing sacrifice to such a blaze.

"I want to look at you." He broke the kiss to make the husky confession. "You're so fucking beautiful. Every inch of you. But I can't seem to let you go."

Placing her hands on his chest, she peeled away from his flesh with reluctance mirroring his own. "I want to look at you, too," she replied from behind lowered lashes. "Perhaps while you discard your trousers and boots, we can become familiar with the sight of each other. And then... we can familiarize ourselves in other ways."

He shook his head, and it took a moment for Felicity to realize it wasn't in rejection of her suggestion, but in incredulity. "A man's body is nothing but a utility, whereas you..." He seemed to lose his ability to speak.

"I want to see," she gently insisted, stepping out of the circle of his arms.

His gaze devoured her as his hands fell to his waistband. Felicity found it rather lovely that he didn't simply stare at her breasts and the thatch of gold between her thighs. Other parts of her seemed to snag his notice. The curve of her shoulder, the dip of her waist, her feet, and her hips.

That wasn't to say his eyes didn't darken with dangerous storms when they devoured the most private parts of her.

Finished with his buttons, he bent to remove his

boots, and Felicity, in kind, hungrily viewed the bunches and planes of his shoulders, the chords of his neck, the ropes and knots of his insanely muscled arms.

Pushing his trousers and underthings down in one motion, he stepped out of them and straightened, standing before her with nothing but the firelight flickering off his magnificence.

All moisture deserted her mouth as his sex, already heavy and large, thickened right before her eyes, swelling against veins and smooth skin.

Swallowing profusely, she did her best to tamp down on a surge of concern. She could think of no place in her body where that could possibly fit.

He'd been wrong about men, though.

At least about himself.

Never in her life had she looked upon something and been so thoroughly affected. Not the art at the Louvre, or the plethora of other monuments made by man or nature.

Gabriel Sauvageau was certainly built with the perfection and precision of the most ingenious of machinery. He rippled with strength, and radiated masculinity.

Every single part of him was so large. So undoubtedly male. His thighs, thick with the divots and swells of detailed muscle. His torso, ribbed and grooved with sinew and strength.

But what truly transfixed her was the art he'd carved into his own skin, often covering scars beneath.

The wary suspicion haunting his eyes moved her as she floated toward him, her hands reaching out to splay across the veritable mounds of his chest. She loved the dichotomy of crisp yet silken hair beneath her smooth palms.

Not a word was spoken as she smoothed her hands up over the mountains of his shoulders and down the slopes of his arms. He stood passively— if not patiently— allowing her to inspect a tattoo she liked, or trail her finger along a scar.

She'd ask about them someday. Each one. When they'd become more comfortable like this. When the uncertainty had given over to trust.

It was cruel to other men, she decided, that one such as he should exist. He was Achilles in a field of Greeks. Some of them heroes, some of them even demigods, perhaps.

And not one with the slightest hope of comparing to him.

"You can touch me, too, if you like," she offered with a bashful flutter of her lashes.

His hands curled to fists at his sides. "Not yet," he said through clenched teeth. "I'm not… in control."

She made a sympathetic sound, wondering if arousal was different for men and women. Because, for the first time in her entire life, she felt nothing less than powerful. It was a strong word, but she hadn't another one in her repertoire.

Fear didn't belong in this place, because he'd chased it away. Of course, she fought a bit of self-conscious uncertainty and her innate shyness and modesty.

But no courage was necessary, because she was truly unafraid. *In* control. She held this beast of a man beneath a spell, and before the night was through, they'd belong to each other.

His gaze upon her was a strange medley of reverent and carnal, and she lifted onto the tips of her toes to offer a kiss.

He still had to bend a little to grant it, and she smiled against his lips when he did.

Relentless in their quest, her fingers slid between them, drawing past the corrugations of his abdomen, and the bandage at his side, to where she knew a delightful trail of dark hair led down to his sex.

"No." He tore his mouth from hers, levering his hips out of reach.

She pulled her hand away, as if she had been branded. "Did I do something wrong?"

Smoothing a rough palm down her hair, he quickly replied, "Never, *mon coeur*. But I am so... if you touch me. I might... I might come."

"That's all right. I don't mind."

"*I mind.*" His brows drew together.

"I'd like to know what it feels like," she admitted. "I'd like to see before..." She ducked her head into his shoulder, her fingers finding a tender, especially smooth spot of skin where his hip met his thigh.

Nodding, he closed his eyes.

Her name escaped his lips on a strangled whisper as she found the barrel of his erection with her smooth, cool fingers.

The heat of it stunned her the most. Though his entire body was flush and warming from the firelight, his cock was like a branding iron, pulsing with warmth.

Clutching her to him, he buried his head into her hair as she explored his sex with careful fingertips and breaths of wonder. Upon finding a large vein beneath, she was delighted to discover that when she fondled it, the entire organ flexed and throbbed, and made a man of his size whimper. She traced the smooth ridge of the head, finding a bead of moisture at the tip, as slick as her own body's response.

When she palmed him, his hips rolled forward with an instinctive glide, thrusting deeper into the circle of her hand.

A moan of agony vibrated against her ear.

Squeezing, testing, she let him slide against her grip, feeling the intimate skin move like velvet over heated steel.

After only a few thrusts, his body tensed, trembled,

and he made the most helpless sound. Something exceptionally low and almost plaintive. His shoulders bunched and arms flexed, though he was careful not to clench her too hard as the flesh in her hand thickened, throbbed, and then released warm and slick pulses against her belly.

He nearly collapsed when she let him go, but he caught himself and shocked her by immediately bending and finding his discarded towel to wipe her skin clean and dry.

After, he plucked her close for a searing kiss, one that tilted the world on its very axis, or so she thought until she felt the familiar softness of her coverlet beneath her shoulder blades.

He'd lowered them to the ground and levered to his side next to her, cradling her head on his arm, leaving his other hand free to mount an expedition of his own.

First, he relieved her of her spectacles, discarding them to the hearth behind him.

Something about the care he took with them touched her in an altogether different way than his fingers did.

"My God," he breathed, his eyes fluttering closed as his fingertips dipped from her jaw to her neck and down to stroke into the divot of her clavicle. "I knew women were soft, but I never... I never could have imagined."

His words pleased her, and yet she felt so exposed like this. So vulnerable and— well— naked. "Is there... Should I be doing something?"

His eyes never opened wider than half-mast as his chuckle rumbled over her like the purr of a lion. "You've done enough, *mon coeur*. Allow me."

It hadn't ever occurred to Felicity that a gaze could feel as intense as a caress, until he dragged it to her breasts, the flesh quivering beneath the taut peaks.

Slowly, his hands followed, trailing down the expanse of her chest. His fingers splayed as they climbed one side of the mound, brushed over the sensitive bud one at a time, and descended down the thin skin beneath.

Felicity tossed her head back and closed her eyes, gasping each time a finger found her nipple, clenching as the sensation traveled from her breast, down her nerves, and landed in her loins.

"Do you like this?" he queried.

She nodded, too attenuated by his motions to form a reply.

Reluctantly, he left her breasts to graze her ribs, lifting goose pimples over her entire body as he tentatively spanned her waist, testing its shape. At the soft curve of her belly, he paused, spreading his palm flat beneath her navel.

Over her womb.

All hesitancy abandoned his gaze then, as a fierce expression overtook his features. One that called to the very primal place inside of her that had responded to him from the very first.

This was a man who would have drawn her desire in any time. If he'd have captained a galleon. Or have been a fearsome knight. Or have donned primitive linens and used rudimentary spears to keep the wolves from their door.

Ages ago, when he could have claimed her as his wife by simply dragging her into his hut and breeding with her. When she could have been expected to be nothing but grateful to find a man capable of protecting her from the brutal elements and the whims of other beasts.

In the days when size and strength was revered over birth and breeding, Gabriel Sauvageau would have been a king.

He'd have been worshiped as a god.

If everything that made their connection complicated to the point of impossible didn't exist, Felicity knew in that moment, he'd not hesitate to plant a child in that place beneath his hand.

An empty yearning opened a chasm there, and her hips undulated restlessly of their own accord.

His gaze snapped to her sex. And stayed there, captured by whatever he saw.

Biting her lip, Felicity fought the urge to squirm as she stared up into his hard, unreadable expression. Was he unimpressed?

"Open for me."

At his whispered, terse command, her thighs parted of their own accord.

The uncontested ferocity in his gaze stole her breath as he glimpsed her intimate flesh for the first time. His tongue darted out to wet his lips, and a flood of arousal drew a soft sound from her throat.

It was all the encouragement he needed.

Erotic sparks shimmered through every inch of her body as his curious fingers petted through the dusting of gold hair, and slid into the passion-soaked folds of her sex.

If Felicity had thought to be embarrassed by the abundant moisture he found there, the dark, ardent sound he made deep in his throat dispelled her of that notion.

It was what he did to her, after all.

Gabriel Sauvageau liquified her with every gentle, clever discovery of his roughened fingers as they parted the seam of her sex, sliding over the pliant ruffles of flesh that protected the entrance to her body.

Instantly, he found the swollen nub at her center and pressed it, causing her to jump and squirm away from an almost painful, electric jolt.

He froze, his eyes going wide with panic. "I hurt you."

"No— that is... it was a touch too strong."

"Should I stop?"

She smoothed at his brow and shook her head, lifting

her hips to meet his hand. Cautiously, he resumed his soft strokes and lazy explorations, watching her every expression so intently, she thought she might die from the tenderness he evoked in her chest.

From the agonizing ache he conjured in her core.

They both learned her pleasure was found if teased around the nub, skipping over it with whisper-soft strokes and shivering thrums.

Felicity felt as if she'd become intoxicated, the world spinning behind her eyes when they closed, drowning in the heat and pure liquid pleasure of the moment.

She'd read about *le petite mort*. The little death. The culmination of sexual pleasure he'd only just found in her hands. And still, as something potent and powerful spun toward her like a whirlwind, threatening to drag her away from herself, she was ashamed to find she panicked a little.

Gripping his shoulders, she gasped his name, which escaped as a question.

"I'm here, *mon amour*," he murmured, nuzzling at her, pressing gentle, tender kisses against her mouth as she writhed and ground against his hand.

He kissed down her neck, her chest, and found her bare breasts with an appreciative groan, reveled there for a moment, dragging his tongue around the puckered flesh of her areola, doing his utmost to keep his stubble from abrading the sensitive nerves.

"Who is your God, Felicity? You are too fucking beautiful to be made of the same clay and dust as the rest of us." His blasphemy was beautiful, and it sang in her bones as he closed his hot mouth around her nipple and laved it with his tongue.

A moan hummed from between her lips as her thighs fell wider of their own accord. His fingers had found the perfect rhythm, and pulled the pinnacle of pleasure from the deepest parts of her.

The spasms engulfed her in wonderous waves of delight, culminating in her core and then spreading through her veins in sparkling surges. Very far away, someone made the most pathetic of noises, mewls and pants and pleas. She barely heard them as the glorious sensations intensified. Her body bowed and arched, pulsing with a pleasure so acute, she worried her muscles might strain to the point of snapping.

Eventually, her body became one raw nerve, and she collapsed, folding her knees up, seeking escape from an abundance of ecstasy.

Only when she returned to herself, did she realize those sounds had been ripped from her own throat.

Feeling more than a little vulnerable, she reared up to tug at him, needing warmth and weight and comfort.

He complied, immediately, cautiously rolling to cover her with agonizing deliberation, draping himself over her, but never settling his weight fully.

Beneath him she melted like a candle that'd spent its entire wick, a puddle of pliant warmth.

It was too easy to luxuriate in his tender care of her as he stroked her hair, dropping featherlight kisses on her brow, her eyelids, her nose. Her cheekbones. The corners of her mouth.

She loved this. Being spread beneath him, her thighs obliged wider to accept his bulk.

And every part that'd been relaxed and released went instantly rigid as the hot brand of his hard sex pressed against her.

He was ready… again.

EVERYTHING THAT MADE GABRIEL A MAN RIPPLED BENEATH his skin at the electrifying contact of his sex and hers. He squeezed his eyes shut in half a wince and half an expression of wonder.

To spend in her hand had been a blessing, as she'd not only released a torrent of the most powerful pleasure he'd yet known, but she'd also released the hold his overwhelming lust had on his brain and body.

But when she'd parted her lovely slim thighs, unveiling the secrets of her body to him, his cock had become painfully full again.

Felicity wasn't the first woman he'd seen in the nude. So much of his business had been done in crude places and alleys where ladies exposed themselves for money, or serviced a man outside with only the shadows to conceal them.

It was good, he supposed, not for the sake of comparison, but because if he'd not had at least a general idea of what existed beneath a woman's dress, the sight of her bare ass when he'd walked into the room might have killed him.

Let alone the rest of her. The alabaster perfection of her peach-tipped breasts. The flush of her smooth skin…

Her sex. Pink, pretty flesh nestled in a feather dusting of dark gold curls.

If he did nothing in his life to be proud of, her pleasure was enough to make him feel like a god. The arch of her sinuous body, the lithe movements of her hips as she rode the waves of her climax.

A climax he'd provided.

He'd meant to keep the evidence of his desire away from her, but his body betrayed him, seeking the warmth only she could provide.

Their gazes clashed when the barrel of his cock settled against the heat of her core. He could still feel the little pulses of her pleasure throbbing in time to the increasing heartbeat surging through his shaft.

Not daring to move, he schooled the need out of his

features. He could think of nothing other than drilling into her like the base and perverse animal he was, but the need was tempered by his regard for her.

His love.

Her eyes had gone heavy and sleepy after she'd come, and her need for his closeness broke his heart into tender shards.

If this was all they did tonight, he was satisfied.

Well… *satisfied* was too strong a word. But he recognized with unquestionable thoroughness just how bloody fortunate he was to have done what they did.

It would never be enough.

Felicity slid her hands around to his back and scorched little paths of fire over the thick bands of muscle. Muscle he was glad he possessed if only to use it in service of her. To keep and protect her. To perform the labor she physically could not, and have the strength and stamina to provide her pleasure.

To keep from crushing her now as her hips pressed gently upward, pressing his cock against that marvelous, pliant skin unique to her sex. Coating him in the slick leavings of her desire. The moisture he'd need to make his way inside of her.

He gazed down at her angelic face, suffused with sheer, incredible wonder.

How did a woman like this exist? How was it possible that he'd not only found her but somehow events had unfolded in such a way, that she was now beneath him, legs spreading wider in unmistakable invitation.

Lowering onto his elbows, he framed her head with his forearms, plunging his fingers into her hair and cradling her scalp from the hard floor beneath the coverlet.

Arching his hips back slightly, it didn't surprise him that the crown of his cock found the entrance to her body without aid, nudging against the moist kiss of taut skin there.

He watched every twitch, every tiny change or tightening in her lovely features. Examined her for fear or pity or any long-suffering.

Not trusting what he found.

The pillows of her lips were plush and red, swollen from his kisses. Her eyes were dark and gleamed with a passion that went beyond permission and into the realm of demand. The color in her cheeks was high and the barest sheen of moisture glinted at her hairline.

I love you.

He wanted to say it as he entered her.

But men in bed were often men in love, and he worried the sincerity would be lost.

It would be cruel to tell her if he was still expected to leave her. If she still needed to marry another in order to fulfil her responsibilities.

That didn't change the truth, however, so he allowed the words to flood him as he pressed forward, breaching her body in slow, excruciating increments.

Encountering a barrier almost immediately, her gasp paralyzed him, as did the shadow of pain pinching her features.

When he would have withdrawn, she seized him, wrapping her arms around his torso and visibly bracing herself. "No. No. Just... ignore my pain."

"I could *never* ignore your pain," he contended. "We don't have to—"

She stopped him with a kiss so tender and certain, he forgot any doubt, until the connection of their bodies was the only sensation he could feel.

"I was made for this," she reminded him, adjusting the angle of her body in a way that pressed the breath from his lungs. "My body is crafted to accept a man. You. I'm asking you not to prolong either of our discomfort. Please. Just—"

Her voice broke on a sob as he thrust forward, impaling her as deep as he could, which seemed to be barely over halfway.

A sweltering slew of expletives burst from him as he held himself utterly still with trembling limbs. He cursed the cruel God who made this the most incredible bliss he could have possibly experienced...

And a terrible sort of discomfort for her.

Her nails bit into his back, and he welcomed the pain, wishing he could take it all from her. Because pain had become his friend over the years. Had often been the only way he'd known he was still alive.

But it didn't belong in her eyes.

"I'm sorry," he groaned, pressing his forehead to hers.

She said nothing, only breathed with him as he'd once taught her to do until he could feel the gradual give of her intimate muscles as her body accepted him inside.

In Gabriel's experience, desire and privation had been his only drive. An emptiness he tried to fill with a fortune nearly consumed him, because with every acquisition, every time he reached for a fantasy... the reality always left him disappointed.

But this. This. Her.

Even though her body only sheathed half of him, the sensations suffusing him were far superior to anything he conjured on the lonely nights he'd spent dreaming of exactly this moment.

With her gentle sigh of relief, her muscles released further, welcoming more of him inside.

"Try again," she urged softly.

He withdrew, gasping at the hot ripples of her intimate flesh as it gripped at his retreating cock, as if reluctant to let him go. He sank in again, gaining a bit more ground. Then again. And once more, until he'd seated himself as far as she seemed to be able to take.

After only those handful of motions, they were both panting and sweating, their chests heaving against the other.

He was inside her. A part of her. Locked within her body and her embrace.

Never in his life had he dared to hope. Christ... He wanted to savor the moment, but a drive as ancient as humanity itself, took his body away from his heart.

Ecstasy overtook pleasure as he found a slow, rippling rhythm with his hips, not withdrawing much at all, merely rocking against her.

Her lips moved with words he couldn't hear over the roaring in his ears, so he dropped his head to her shoulder, releasing a shuddering breath. Fighting the rapture already clawing up his spine.

Her soundless whispers of encouragement never permeated the words that created a percussion to his every thrust.

Gold hair. Blue gaze. Soft smile. Scents. Blooms. Spice. Herbs. Slick musk. Smooth flesh.

He felt like a prisoner set free. Or perhaps better, like a warrior invited home.

Home.

That word had never meant anything to him until now.

Welcoming the mindless lust threatening to take over his emotive thoughts, Gabriel found the slick sounds their bodies made incredibly erotic, and he had to focus on keeping himself sane.

Lifting onto his hands to check on her, he nearly lost his rhythm at the sight. If she'd been breathtaking before, looking at her now was like trying to gaze at the sun.

He marveled as she seemed to lose control of her limbs, writhing beneath him, twitching and trembling, clutching at him with artless demands. Her hand smoothed down his back, lower, to shyly explore the curve of his ass, pressing him forward, deeper.

Without thought, he repositioned a bit, his cock finding some deep-seated place inside her that peeled her eyes wide.

"There," she gasped. "Don't stop."

He would never. Instead, he accelerated his pace, deepened his strokes, driving himself home. Inside of her, he could feel the muscles quicken, tighten and release in unbearably sweet spasms as she opened her mouth in a soundless scream.

His own cock thickened, and he held on for as long as he possibly could before, with a deep groan of regret and iron will, he retracted from her, his seed spilling onto the ground beneath her open legs as his entire body undulated with inexhaustible, all-encompassing bliss.

Though the temptation to remain joined with her haunted him in the moments after the storm had passed, Gabriel noted the absolution of exhaustion in the sprawl of her limbs.

Her eyes were languorous upon his as she fought some sort of oblivion with a soft smile and a sigh that turned into a jaw-cracking yawn.

Finding that a torpor also called to him, Gabriel lifted her and took her to bed, pulling the remaining covers over her body.

"Stay?" she murmured, her eyes already closed as if she knew as well as he did that he couldn't deny her.

All he wanted was to sleep with her, but something about it almost felt too much.

Too intimate.

More permanent and unretractable even, than what they'd just done.

Lifting the covers, he slid into the bed beside her, gathering her close as she turned to curl into his body.

In seconds, her breath had steadied, and her lashes had begun to flutter with dreams.

Gabriel's heart wouldn't allow him to sleep for a long time. It beat a tattoo against his chest, four syllables at a time. Her name.

Felicity.

Happiness. Joy. Completion.

Never had a name been so perfect.

CHAPTER 15

Felicity would have loved nothing more than to spend the rest of the day in bed with Gabriel, discovering what his broad body looked like when the drapes were thrown open to the daylight.

Against the snow-white cloud of her bed, he was surely a wicked, colorful mélange of ink and flesh and muscle and sex.

But, alas, Mercy had pounded on her door just after dawn— demanding to know why it was locked— and then harassed her into meeting them downstairs for breakfast.

They'd an attempted-murderer to catch, after all.

Felicity might have rolled out of bed, if Gabriel hadn't caught her first, pulling her bottom back against his hips.

She gasped as his erection throbbed against the cleft, then moaned as his lips found her ear and nibbled it.

Responding instantly, she rolled her hips, delighted when his cock slid between her thighs from behind.

Filthy French words spilled from his sleep-husked voice as his hand glided around to cup her breasts before angling down her belly to delve into her slit.

Lifting her leg for him to gain access, Felicity covered her mouth and bit down on her palm as he simultaneously slid into her from behind and worked damp circles around the hood of her sex with his clever fingers.

Her climax was less a climb to the stars as it was an explosion of them, and she had to bite the pad of her palm in order to not scream the house down now that it was awake.

As her clenching spasms began to abate, he quickened his strokes, the hand in her hair curling into a fist as he pulled out of her body and thrust between her thighs lubricated by the slick jets of his release.

He barely took the time to regain any breath before he left for the basin and returned with a damp cloth.

It was this thoughtfulness that made her care for him so. How strange, for a man so adverse to being vulnerable, who hid himself from everyone, to walk naked in her room with the prowling confidence of a rutting stag.

She liked it.

"There's something I want to tell you," he said once she'd been administered to.

"What's that?" Sitting up, she nuzzled into his neck.

"Your sister is the worst."

She giggled at his mock-aggrieved expression, playfully pushing him out of her bed with a shove of her foot.

"Better you go and dress in your own chamber, before Mrs. Pickering finds you in here and forces you to make an honest woman of me."

She'd said it in jest, but their gazes crashed together for an uneasy moment. Her words landing on the floor in a heap of disorganized chaos between them.

They'd never spoken of the future.

Swallowing, Felicity was the first to give into her cowardice. "I-I'll see you at breakfast."

"Of course."

They didn't look at each other as he gathered his clothing and left.

Felicity was hoping the awkwardness between them

would dispel by breakfast, but it hung above them like a sword through the meal. And then in the carriage after, when they went to the offices of George C. White, Esquire, to question her father's solicitor.

Finding the offices suspiciously vacant, they followed a strange and complicated trail through the city, finally determining that Mr. White had left the country for an indeterminate amount of time.

It was well into the afternoon by then, and they all decided to return to Cresthaven for luncheon to plot their next move.

"Actually," Mercy said as the carriage pulled into the courtyard. "I have a friend through the Eddard Sharpe Society of Homicidal Mystery Analysis who might know how to find this Marco Villanueve. He's always talking about his contacts in the smuggling world." She reached out and squeezed Felicity's knee through her voluminous sage skirts. "What say Rafe and I go pay him a visit while you rest, dear. You look absolutely knackered."

"A lovely idea," Felicity agreed, offering her sister a wan and grateful smile.

"Yes," Raphael agreed, his dark eyebrow lifted at his sullen brother. "That would give you time to talk about whatever is going on between the two of you, I think. I've been wanting to squirm out of my skin all afternoon."

Mercy stepped on his toe and he merely grinned. "Ever the subtle rogue, my husband," she muttered, though her eyes were fond as she gazed over at him.

Emitting a sigh from deep in his chest, Gabriel heaved out of the carriage and held his hand out for Felicity.

A hand that had pleasured her out of her mind just this morning.

Taking it, she stepped down and led the way into the house as the driver turned the carriage in the tight courtyard and clopped back into the mild London afternoon.

"Will you come with me to the parlor?" she asked.

He nodded, his stony expression never changing.

Are you having regrets? She wanted to ask him. *Are you feeling guilty because you are still going to leave?*

What would it take for him to stay?

Because if there was a price, she'd be willing to pay it.

Even if it meant losing everything to gain his heart.

"Gabriel, I—"

Without preamble, he seized her roughly and shoved her behind him, his finger held to his mouth in a signal for silence.

The knife he kept against his back appeared in his hand as he cocked his ear toward her father's study.

Felicity could hear nothing above her racing heart, but she trusted his senses and was happy to allow him to stalk to the door like an advancing buccaneer, ready to slice their intruder to shreds.

Shoving the door open, he lowered the knife immediately, though his grave frown remained firmly in place.

"Mrs. Winterton," he said in a bemused voice. "I think you need to explain yourself."

Gasping, Felicity shimmied past him through the doorframe to see her friend and companion frozen over her father's desk, papers clutched in her hand.

She'd never looked so terrible. Her gold dress hung from a frame that'd become alarmingly thin in the matter of only several days. Her eyes, so lively and blue, had sunken into pallid skin that seemed to all but sag from tired bones. Hair usually the lambent color of copper escaped a hasty knot in limp, dull strands. The papers in her hands shook, and she let them fall to the desk to wring her fingers together.

Moving as if her joints hurt, Emmaline Winterton turned to Felicity with lashes gathered in spikes as tears leaked out the corner of her eyes. "I'm so sorry," she all but croaked. "I didn't mean for any of this to happen. You have to believe that—"

"Oh, do shut up, you dull bitch."

The moment the masculine voice slithered from around the other side of the door, Felicity could feel Gabriel surge behind her, moving to place himself in between her and the interloper.

Something stopped him.

Looking behind her, Felicity despaired to find that a thin metal garrote had been slipped around his neck by a cutthroat, and two other burly brutes had ahold of each straining arm.

His knife clattered to the floor. A furious roar became a choked groan as the weapon cut into his windpipe, strangling his breath.

"No." Felicity reached toward him, only to have her elbow seized by a clawlike hand that jerked her off her feet and tossed her against the desk.

She whimpered as her hip caught the edge, but wrenched her hand away when Emmaline reached for her.

Facing her enemy, she was astonished to find him a perfect stranger.

Though his suit was at least a year or more out of fashion, it might have been expensive once. It stretched over a paunch that'd increased significantly since the initial tailoring of his vest and jacket. Grey hair was pulled back into a queue over a face that might have belonged to a raven in another life, it was so beakish and gaunt.

"You let these men into my house?" she accused Mrs. Winterton, gagging on her first bitter taste of true betrayal.

"Oh, don't be too hard on our Emmaline." The man tapped on the desk with a heavy cane, causing Emmaline to flinch. "I didn't give her much of a choice."

She glanced from Emmaline to her assailant to Gabriel, as her terror spiked.

Gabriel's face had gone red, but at least his chest was

heaving with breath now, which was all that mattered. He had saved her life so many times.

Now she must return the favor.

She attuned her breaths to his, focusing her mind on the intruder in front of her. If she could provide him what he wanted, perhaps he'd leave them unharmed.

"She's not my Emmaline," Felicity said evenly. "Why did she bring you here, and what will it take for you to leave?"

At that, his comically thin eyebrows crawled up to where his hairline might have once been in his younger days. "Oh, but she is your Emmaline. She is *my* Emmaline. We all belong to each other, my dear. Because we're family." Pulling back the hem of his coat, he showed her a pistol, but his remark had already landed like a bullet to her middle.

"A-are you M.W. Goode?" Felicity asked, dreading an answer that would make this man her blood relative in any fashion.

He brightened, his boots clicking together as he tapped an idea out of the air. "Oh yes, introductions." He gave her a comically chivalrous bow. "I am Sir Reginald Winterton III, and my elder sister, Mary, was your father's legal wife and Baroness."

Felicity's heart slammed against its cage as she gaped at him. "You're lying."

"I wish I were," he scoffed. "But decades ago, before your mother came along, Clarence and my sister, Mary, eloped to Gretna Green and were wed. I've brought along the license to prove it. But poor Mary's dowry was not what your father wanted for them, and so they hatched a plan. He'd wed a wealthy invalid heiress— your mother— and stash his true love and wife— my sister, Mary— in the country until the woman gave up the ghost, leaving her fortune to him."

He meandered to one of the bookcases above which a

framed portrait of the Baron and Baroness Cresthaven loomed over the room.

Looming had once been her father's favorite pastime.

"Unfortunately, the life of a Baroness agreed with your mother, and she regained her good health. Your father formed an attachment, resulting in you four girls."

Felicity shook her head, staring into the ice blue eyes of her father's rendering, eyes he'd passed on to her… and to Emmaline? "My father was… a bigamist?"

Sir Reginald's lip curled into an ugly snarl. "He thrust upon Mary the life of a mistress, turning his true bride into nothing better than a whore, and his true-born children into bastards."

Felicity turned to Emmaline, the woman who'd lived in her house since before her parents had died. Tears streaked down the woman's colorless cheeks, though her expression remained as smooth and bleak as the grave.

"Our father turned our own half-sister into our governess?" she asked, horrified. "He installed you in our home and bade you keep such a secret?"

Clarence Goode had been a cold and ruthless man. A miser, a zealot, and, she was ashamed to say, a bigot, but she'd never expected him to be so cruel to his own children.

Indifferent, yes. But this…

"Uncle Reginald had been blackmailing him since Mother died of cancer," Emmaline said with little inflection.

"Your father was a cheapskate!" Reginald crowed, thumping his cane against the floor.

Felicity was beginning to hate that cane, and from the way Emmaline warily avoided it, she suspected the poor woman had greater reason to do so.

"So long as his precious *Mary* was alive, he kept us in the manner which befitted our stations." Reginald's acrimony escaped on every syllable, along with a good bit of spittle. "But once she'd gone, his upkeep dwindled. He began trying to arrange marriages for the children to get them settled, and bestowed upon them dowries and educations rather than liquid money." He stalked closer to her. "How were we supposed to live in the meantime, I ask you?"

Felicity blinked up at him, stalled on one particular thing he'd said.

"Children?" She glanced at Emmaline. "There are more of you?"

Emmaline's eyes hardened to chips of ice. "A younger brother, Emmett, and a younger sister, Rosaline, whom Uncle Reginald keeps as his ward. Indeed, she does not come of age until she is twenty-one. But after I visited her that day I was poisoned, I found her in terrible straits. I do not know if she will survive another year."

"Don't you whisper a breath of those ugly rumors, Emma," he sneered. "Or you won't like what I'm forced to do to defend myself."

A darkness in his voice threaded a peculiar revulsion through Felicity's blood. It took all her sparse courage to face him. "I ask you again to tell me what it is you want. Is it money? You shall have it, but only if you release my personal guard."

His dark eyes twinkled a bit, and he seemed to relax, though he made no motion to release Gabriel.

Felicity couldn't say she blamed him, from the pure murder etched onto her lover's harsh features, any idiot in Blighty would be aware he was not safe.

Reginald retrieved a large envelope of papers from a case. "I have the marriage certificate, the proof of the children's progeny, and correspondence and documents that demonstrate what your father has done. I sent Emma here to find and retrieve the deed to Fairhaven, but she has failed to do so. Then old Clarence went and died, leaving his entire fortune to you. *You*? The youngest and least deserving of his bastards. That, I could not abide."

"He tried to force me to ruin you." Emmaline spoke a bit stronger now, as if she, too, had summoned courage against her tormenter. "To find what you had and take everything. But I loved you all so much. I stayed because I felt safe here. Because I couldn't bring myself to hurt you, Felicity, most of all." She dropped her head into her hands. "And poor Rosaline and Emmett have suffered for my selfishness. When I learned of their misery, I began to acquiesce to his despicable demands. It was *me* who left that threatening note in your parlor, but it was written by his hand. I had no notion that he'd go so far as to try and poison you."

"That was only after my attempt to kidnap you and make you disappear failed," Reginald muttered with a put-upon sigh. "Better it look like an accident, like you ingested one of your own plants."

A low growl emitted from Gabriel's direction, but Felicity forced herself not to look. If she saw him in pain, her strength would abandon her.

"You want me dead," she realized. "So, the fortune will go to the true-born heir."

Emmett. She turned the name over in her mind. She'd a brother. Her father had sired an heir after all, but with the wrong woman.

It must have galled him every day.

"I only want what's best for my nieces and nephew, so that my wards have legal claim to their rightful inheritance, and I, as their guardian, will guide them as I see fit."

"Is Emmett in his minority?" she asked.

"No." Reginald wrinkled his nose in distaste as a shudder coursed through him. "He is quite seven-and-twenty. I had him institutionalized, poor boy, for his unnatural urges, until Emmaline began to cooperate."

"Institutionalized?"

"He's... unnatural." Reginald bared his teeth. "An invert."

Felicity held a hand to her lips. She'd heard of inverts; they were men who preferred the romantic company of other men... She couldn't imagine shutting them up in a hellish asylum. "My God. He's not still there, is he?"

"He's recovering... for now. It was all quite terrible for him." Reginal sidled closer to her. "It's nearly impossible to afford his upkeep now, without his inheritance. He might have to go back."

Swamped with grief for siblings she'd never met, Felicity rushed to the bookshelf and retrieved the Bible, flipping through the gold-leaf pages to retract the deed. "I can give you Fairhaven. For that matter, I can give you Cresthaven if you want it. You can name your sum, if only..." She searched her mind for a solution. "If you'll relinquish the guardianship of my siblings to me."

He laughed as his pistol appeared, wiping a tear of mirth from the corner of his eye. "Why would I settle for a sum, when I can have the entire thing?"

Panic threatened to overwhelm her as her limbs went numb. "I-If that gun goes off in this neighborhood, the bobbies come running. There's no getting away with this."

"You think I haven't considered everything?" he smirked.

She cast desperately about for another threat. "Also... Mercy and Raphael will be here any moment."

"I already have men lying in wait at the door." He pulled paperwork from his pocket. "You're going to marry me, Felicity Goode; whether it's before or after you die is your decision."

"You didn't bring enough men," came Gabriel's throaty growl from the doorway.

"I brought plenty, it seems," Reginald remonstrated,

gesturing to the three men who kept the monstrous gangster at bay.

Felicity did her best to draw Reginald's focus away from Gabriel. He'd already been shot once defending her, she couldn't allow that again. "You know Chief Inspector Carlton Morley will never let this hold. You don't understand the dynamics of this family. We're very close. They'll know any sort of marriage is a sham. They'll fight you in court. They'll find you out and see you hanged for murder."

"You're not going to live long enough to hang." Gabriel's threat was so feral, she almost believed him.

"Come again?" With a snap of Reginald's fingers, the garrote tightened once more, cutting off Gabriel's ability to speak.

To add insult to injury, the man on his right moved to block the doorway. Hauling a hammer-sized fist back, he punched Gabriel hard enough to crack his head to the side.

He barely blinked, merely turned his head back to stare at the man with lips pressed tightly closed.

Reginald resumed his threats. "I will dismantle this undeserving dynasty built by a man who broke his word to us. Starting with you and your twin, and working my way up to the top of Scotland Yard. Then all of this will go to the rightful family..." He swept his arms to encompass the entirety of Cresthaven Place. "Or..." He looked at her out of the sides of his eyes, revealing whites tinged a disgusting shade of yellow.

"Or what?" Felicity couldn't stop herself from asking, though she was certain she would detest his response.

"Or... You marry me in earnest. And what's yours becomes mine."

"It won't work," she informed him. "The will stipulates I have to marry above a viscount."

"There are ways around such stipulations." Reaching

out, he drew a finger across Felicity's jaw, then traced the edge of her collar down the line of her throat.

In that moment, Gabriel Sauvageau spit a mouthful of blood into the eyes of the man who'd struck him, then snapped his head back to break the nose of the man with the death grip on the garrote.

Reginald swiveled around, but before he leveled his pistol at Gabriel, Felicity seized his cane from his left hand and struck out at the wrist with which he held the weapon.

A few well-placed elbows saw Gabriel freed, and when he dipped to gather the knife from the floor, he turned to her, swiping a drop of red from the corner of his mouth.

"Turn away, *mon coeur*," he said, his eyes dark with a strange amalgamation of regret and anticipation as he advanced on Reginald, kicking away the pistol.

Felicity obeyed. She dashed around the desk to Emmaline, who collapsed against her. They clung to each other, staring into the fireplace, not once looking back even as terrible sounds reached them.

Felicity didn't have to ask why he'd directed her not to look.

He didn't want her to see all the blood he spilt.

CHAPTER 16

In a matter of hours, it was as if no one had died in the house.

Felicity realized that when one had a gangster, a surgeon, and a chief inspector in one's family, one never had to worry about divesting oneself of bodies.

On pure chance, Raphael and Mercy had returned moments after the violence, having forgotten Mercy's case notebook.

Gabriel had barely helped Felicity and Emmaline navigate the carnage and collapse into the parlor, when her brother-in-law strode onto the scene looking like the devil's own butler, one hand gripping his lapel like a chuffed politician. "I say, *mon frere*, do you have any idea why I was forced to kill two men at the courtyard door?"

Mercy was much less collected as she shoved past the Sauvageau brothers and dashed to her side. "Dear God! Felicity, Mrs. Winterton, are you all right?"

Astonished that she'd held together this long, Felicity began to quake with bone-deep shudders. And still, she was able to turn and take the freezing fingers of the woman sitting beside her. "Mercy, meet Emmaline, our sister."

After a flurry of action in the middle of which Emmaline and Felicity sat leaning on each other, siblings and spouses were called upon, and arrangements, both legal and otherwise, cleared their house of all evidence of violence.

Now Felicity sat surrounded by her family, squirming beneath their expectant regard.

Everyone had a strong drink in their hands, including herself. Morley and Prudence stood by the fireplace, helping themselves to whisky brought by a subdued Mr. Bartholomew.

Titus, who'd once shoveled the coal used to light said fireplace, pulled a comfortable chair in front of it, and settled his very pregnant wife, Honoria, into it. Propping her swollen feet on a stool and covering her lap with a blanket, he hovered protectively, attentive to any need that might arise.

Mercy sat on the other side of Emmaline, and Raphael hitched one leg against the armrest next to her, half-leaning, half-sitting as he sipped a glass of red wine.

As per usual, Gabriel— who took up the most room— lurked in the shadows by the doorway, silent and grim as a reaper.

Felicity found herself afraid he would slip away if she didn't keep checking on him. He'd changed his clothing, securing his collar very high to his chin, concealing what she was certain to be an ugly line around his throat.

She wanted to see it. To make Titus examine it.

She wanted him to look at her.

Nora, the eldest, was doing her best to digest the story by asking Emmaline gentle questions. "So, this Sir Reginald… He was your mother's brother, and not a blood relative of ours at all."

Emmaline nodded, sipping some hot tea splashed with brandy. "He is— was— a monster. He consistently threatened my brother. *Our* brother, who is a kind and tender soul. He dragged me this morning from the hospital with threats against not only him but Rosaline, as well. You see, he had... unnatural affections toward her. And Father did nothing."

"He was not a man who cared for the comfort or happiness of his children," Honoria said around a tight swallow, remembering, no doubt, that he'd callously married her off to a violent, criminal viscount.

Emmaline nodded her head in agreement, lips pinched against both physical and emotional pain. "Our father provided us extraordinarily little upkeep after he found out about Emmett's... proclivities. He left instructions for us to find people to marry and care for us. Uncle Reginald had been leaching off Mother ever since she'd fallen ill with the cancer, pretending to the world that he was the one helping us."

"Why did he decide to call you Mrs. Winterton?" Honoria placed an idle hand on her round belly, her ebony brows drawn together. "Are you married?"

"No, but I am ruined," she answered honestly, her pale cheeks regaining some color in the semblance of a blush. "There was a... proposal— it doesn't matter— Father decided that if I was Mrs. Winterton, it lent me respectability and people who even noticed me would be too polite to inquire whether I was a widow or estranged." She let out a beleaguered sigh.

"It is such an injustice that we are slaves to the whims of such men as these," Mercy said vehemently, glaring at everyone in the room guilty of claiming the opposite sex. "I'm glad you are rid of this Reginald. And our father, all told, he treated you most abominably."

Emmaline shook her head with an incredulous expression while she self-consciously did her best to tuck her unruly hair back into the knot it wanted to escape. "I can't apologize enough to you all. I wish I could fix the damage I've done. Especially to you, Felicity, for the danger I brought to your door."

Setting her teacup down with a clatter, she grasped Felicity's hands and held her gaze with one comprised of tears and trepidation. "Thank you for being kind. I understand if you want to throw me out with the rest of the rubbish, but I wanted you to know that you are one of the best people I've ever had the privilege of knowing, and I will always be grateful for the times we shared."

When she would have pulled her hands away, Felicity gripped them tighter. "You're not rubbish. You're family."

Everyone made gentle noises of agreement, which caused the tears gathered in Emmaline's auburn lashes to spill over onto her cheeks. "I suppose I need to return to Fairhaven and inform Rose and Emmett that they are free... finally free." The word produced a watery smile.

"Tell them you are all part of the Goode family now," Felicity said, a decision firmly solidifying in her mind. "And bring Emmett here, of course, so that he might take his seat as the Master of Cresthaven and the proprietor of father's shipping empire."

At that, everyone started talking at once.

"Let's not be hasty—"

"We've never even met—"

"What are you going to do if you give away everything—"

"Felicity, perhaps we should discuss this before you—"

Putting up a hand, she waited until they'd fell into an astounded silence. "There's nothing to discuss, I am quite resolved. If I failed to marry into nobility, Father made unerringly clear that I get nothing and the next in line gets everything. However, if Reginald did one thing, it was to bring to this house evidence of an heir. A true heir. All this should have been his in the first place."

"It does not seem right that you end up with nothing to your name," Raphael noted, playing his role as the devil's advocate. "I think we are well aware that evidence can disappear."

"Yes, but the truth does not," Felicity stated firmly. "And I don't have nothing, I have all of you." She squeezed Emmaline's hand. "And more, besides."

"You can stay with us, of course," Titus offered. "Nora would be so glad of the company, especially once the child arrives."

"Or she lives around the corner with us," Prudence interjected. "Caro and Lottie already adore her, and there's decidedly less blood at our estate than in the hospital. And room for a garden out back."

Mercy snorted. "If you are not taken in by our sisters' obvious ploys to turn you into the spinster aunt who helps them wrangle their unruly children, you are welcome aboard the yacht with Rafe and me. We can have the adventures we always planned." Smiling brilliantly, her twin twinkled mischievous eyes at her sisters, confident she'd won Felicity's favor.

"Or you can stay in your home," Emmaline murmured, with her heart shining in her eyes. "I think you would love being here with family… If Emmett is to be the patriarch, I assure you there is no brother dearer than he is. He will revel in his duty to dote on and care for you."

"*No.*" The one deep, cutting syllable sliced through the swell of love and sentiment in the room as Gabriel stepped from the shadows, his features set as if ready to do battle.

"She is mine. *I* will care for her."

CHAPTER 17

Gabriel's teeth slammed shut after inadvertently speaking the words that his heart had shoved into his throat and out of his mouth.

Peace erupted into chaos again as three men surged to their feet, and as if with one mind, created a line of muscle and masculine challenge between where Gabriel stood and Felicity's chaise.

Even his brother took an uneasy stance against him, scrutinizing him with the eyes of someone who knew all of his sins.

He couldn't blame any of them, they'd just cleaned up the corpses he'd left strewn about the house.

For her.

Their shoulders blocked her perfect features from view, and he wanted more than anything to see her response.

God, he hadn't even asked her what she wanted. He'd just claimed her like some bloody barbarian marauder claimed his spoils of war.

But she had to know she was so much more than that.

Sharing a bed was a great deal different than sharing a life, and the mention of it that morning had been hanging like the sword of Damocles over his head all day.

Because he'd wanted it so much, and knew she'd made other decisions already.

They'd never spoken of what a future between them might look like... but he'd been in love with her since the first night she'd reluctantly assisted Honoria Goode with the clandestine mission that'd brought them into each other's lives.

Raphael had also been struck by Mercy at the beginning, but Gabriel...

He'd been devastated by Felicity.

She'd been his in his heart, his imagination, his every decision since that day.

He knew it was pathetic, and he didn't give a dusty fuck.

He lived and died by her word.

Raphael stepped forward, his eyes both cautious and contrite. "Gabriel... you cannot just announce that—"

"Let him speak." Felicity shouldered through Titus and Morley, attracting all attention in the room.

A spark ignited in his chest. One he'd thought had been extinguished forever.

Hope.

In that moment, everyone else in the room disappeared.

"Felicity. Even though I lied to you about my name, I was honest when I said I'd only known violence. I'd thought people were only capable of malice and greed, cruelty and guile."

Lifting a hand, he caressed her cheek with the backs of his scarred knuckles. "But your goodness— your light— it beckons me. It humbles me. It makes me want to twist myself into you. To tear the parts of myself away that offend you and see them crushed beneath the heel of your boot so that I might weave something better into my tattered soul."

Her mouth dropped open, but he forged ahead,

needing to spill his entire heart before she either accepted or condemned him.

"I'm in love with you," he blurted. "I wish I could undo all the evil that I've done for your sake. I have been a liar and a thief. I am a bastard in every sense of the word. But my feelings for you are the truest thing in me. They are... the sweetest, most tender kind of violence because they have broken me down and shattered everything I thought was the truth.

"I know I said that you were mine but... I don't want to possess you." He held up his hand. "No, that's not true. I can't help but ache to make you mine. Because you *are* mine. Even if you decide that this isn't to be. My heart. My body. My protection. My life. It's yours. I am yours. Even if you gave your future to another. You are still mine, because you are a part of me. The only part of me I can stand."

When he looked up, she was not the only Goode sister with tears streaming down her cheeks.

She covered his hand with hers, turning her cheek into his palm and pressing a gentle kiss to the pads beneath his fingers. "Gabriel. Your past doesn't matter to me. I don't care what man you were. Only the one you are now. The one you will choose to be."

He stepped closer, his eagerness too apparent. "I could be good, if you taught me how."

"She's the only Goode sister who actually deserves the designation," one of the men said in a caustic tone.

Prudence slapped her husband's arm and a chuckle washed the room of some of its gravitas.

Gabriel gathered her hands in his own, and did something he'd never done for man nor God in his entire life.

He knelt. "Marry me? I have no title to offer you—"

"But he's as rich as Midas," Raphael interjected helpfully.

Gabriel shot his brother a withering look. "If you do

not mind that I cannot make you a lady, that we will belong in very few ballrooms, I'll do my best to give you a good life. I'll treat you like a queen. I'll worship you like a goddess. Even though I am broken, I—"

Felicity astonished him by sinking down with him. "You are not broken… you are beautiful," she insisted. "You have become everything to me in such a short time, my entire world seems filled with you." Her lashes swept down as he held his breath, waiting for the answer she seemed ready to give.

"I… only feel safe when I'm with you. But I don't need you to worship me, Gabriel, I don't want to fall off this pedestal I'm on. Because, I'm the broken one. And I have no real reason to be. My fretting will drive you mad, if my snoring doesn't first. I have those fits— those spasms of helpless terror that make no sense and reduce me to nothing without warning. My greatest enemy is often my own mind, the one thing you can't protect me from."

"But I can," he interjected. "I will. I will hold you when you're terrified. I'll remind you that you're safe. I'll help you battle your nightmares, and I'll dig in the garden next to you until they abate. I'll face the world when you cannot. Because, Felicity, the only thing I fear is living a life without you in it."

He couldn't say if he bent to her or she surged up to him, but their lips met in an ecstatic clash, their arms encircled each other with the exuberance of two people finding treasure they'd never even dreamed to possess.

When Gabriel had decided that his heart couldn't expand beyond his encompassing love for the woman in his arms.

He opened his eyes and looked across the room and realized immediately how mistaken he was.

Because he'd have to make room for the entire Goode family.

His family.

EPILOGUE

Felicity woke Christmas morning vibrating with the anticipation of a child. Cosseted in her sleeping husband's grasp, she was torn between squirming away from it, or delving deeper into the warmth and letting the presents be unwrapped without them.

A layer of lacy frost impeded her view from the window, but a steady whistle of wind told her the morning was deliciously stormy, just as predicted.

Oh, sod it. She had to get up. Breakfast would be decadent, and someone had to see the tree lit.

Besides, Gabriel and Raphael said they never really celebrated Christmas, and she'd spent hundreds of hours and a small fortune to make certain this was the most festive holiday in the history of Christendom.

Slipping her fingers around his wrists, she lifted his heavy arm with no small amount of effort and with the agility of an acrobat, slid from beneath it.

Just when she was about free, he made a juvenile sound of protest, and somehow she found herself right back where she'd started.

"Unhand me, you," she giggled. "There's Christmas to be had."

"But Christmas is cold, and it's warm in here. How am I going to tear myself away from you?" He burrowed in deeper, both sharing and taking her warmth.

"I promise it'll be worth it." She squirmed against his unrelenting grip as he rooted in her hair to nuzzle at her cheek. "Just wait until you've seen what I ordered for breakfast. Aren't you hungry?"

"I know what I'd like to feast upon." He nibbled at the sensitive hollow of her ear.

However, his stomach made a rude sound, and hers answered in kind.

"There, you see?" Her finger crumpled against muscle as she poked him in the abdomen. "Your body needs sustenance if you are to keep up your vigor."

"I've had no complaints from you about my vigor." He pressed the evidence of said vigor against her thighs.

Indeed, they'd spent months making up for lost time. In his case, in ways that could only be described as vigorous.

Or perhaps voracious.

Regardless of the word, there were days she found walking difficult.

"Come on, darling," she tugged at him. "I think we should at least face our siblings, yes, since we're all gathered together."

With a plaintive groan, he flopped his glorious body over, quite like a toddler, landing splayed on his back. "It's only that you have so many." He yawned.

Felicity giggled and climbed on top of him, stretching her naked body against his hard frame, knowing she was helping her cause not at all as he purred up at her.

Had a husband ever been so dear? Had two people ever fit into each other's lives so exceedingly, effortlessly well?

Because of their natures, both so solicitous, so in need of ease and comfort and soft, quiet moments, life so far had been something of a respite punctuated by bouts of lovemaking and travel.

They'd joined Raphael and Mercy on the Duchesse de la Cour's yacht, and had lounged in luxury with nothing to look at but endless blue ocean. They'd splayed on Mediterranean beaches, and strolled through Japanese gardens.

Someday soon, they'd find a place to settle. They'd be still somewhere long enough to plant a garden. But for now, they were both content to discover the world, and each other, in languorous time.

Felicity traced her favorite of his tattoos, a potion bottle with her name inside it, right over his heart. "What say you, we join the family for breakfast and presents, and then when everyone adjourns to the stables for a brisk mid-morning ride, we'll do the same."

He filled his hands with the globes of her ass, blowing his lips out with a distinctly equine noise. "But you are afraid of riding horses."

"I wasn't anticipating riding a horse..." She rolled her hips against his length.

His lids went down, and his grip tightened. "Woman, you're playing a dangerous game."

"Am I? Perhaps you're the one in danger." She lifted herself over him, stretching and arching in a way she knew drove him wild.

"Here I was, thinking I'd married an angel, when really you're nothing better than a wicked, insatiable tease." He gave her rear a gentle slap.

Retaliating, she tweaked his nipple and he laughed, playfully covering his chest like a woman whose breasts were exposed.

"You poor, tormented soul," she pouted, wriggling away from him and dancing out of his grip as he levered up and made a grab for her. "How will you ever survive me?"

"I don't mean to survive you, wife," he growled, throwing the covers away from his delectable body. "I mean to devour you."

"Excellent." She winked at him from the washroom doorway. "You can start after breakfast."

ALSO BY KERRIGAN BYRNE

A Goode Girls Romance

Seducing a Stranger

Courting Trouble

Dancing With Danger

Tempting Fate

The Earl of Christmas Past

The Business of Blood Series

The Business of Blood

A Treacherous Trade

A Vocation of Violence

Victorian Rebels

The Highwayman

The Hunter

The Highlander

The Duke

The Scot Beds His Wife

The Duke With the Dragon Tattoo

The MacLauchlan Berserkers

Highland Secret

Highland Shadow

Highland Stranger

To Seduce a Highlander

The MacKay Banshees

Highland Darkness

Highland Devil

Highland Destiny

To Desire a Highlander

The de Moray Druids

Highland Warlord

Highland Witch

Highland Warrior

To Wed a Highlander

Contemporary Suspense

A Righteous Kill

Also by Kerrigan

The Highwayman

The Hunter

The Highlander

The Duke

The Scot Beds His Wife

The Duke With the Dragon Tattoo

How to Love a Duke in Ten Days

All Scot And Bothered

ABOUT THE AUTHOR

Kerrigan Byrne is the USA Today Bestselling and award winning author of THE DUKE WITH THE DRAGON TATTOO. She has authored a dozen novels in both the romance and mystery genre. Her newest mystery release THE BUSINESS OF BLOOD is available October 24th, 2019

She lives on the Olympic Peninsula in Washington with her dream boat husband. When she's not writing and researching, you'll find her on the water sailing and kayaking, or on land eating, drinking, shopping, and taking the dogs to play on the beach.

Kerrigan loves to hear from her readers! To contact her or learn more about her books, please visit her site: www.kerriganbyrne.com